The Naughty Princess

Also From Claire Contreras

The Sinful King
The Wicked Prince – coming soon!
The Consequence of Falling
The Player
Kaleidoscope Hearts
Paper Hearts
Elastic Hearts
The Wilde One
Then There Was You
Fake Love
Half Truths
Twisted Circles
There is No Light in Darkness
Darkness Before Dawn
Because You're Mine

The Naughty Princess

A Sexy Royals Novella

By Claire Contreras

1001 DARK NIGHTS
PRESS

The Naughty Princess
A Sexy Royals Novella
By Claire Contreras

1001 Dark Nights

Published by 1001 Dark Nights Press, an imprint of Evil Eye Concepts, Incorporated

Sign up for the 1001 Dark Nights Newsletter
and be entered to win a Tiffany Key necklace.

There's a contest every month!

Go to www.1001DarkNights.com to subscribe.

**As a bonus, all subscribers can download
FIVE FREE exclusive books!**

One Thousand and One Dark Nights

Once upon a time, in the future...

*I was a student fascinated with stories and learning.
I studied philosophy, poetry, history, the occult, and
the art and science of love and magic. I had a vast
library at my father's home and collected thousands
of volumes of fantastic tales.*

*I learned all about ancient races and bygone
times. About myths and legends and dreams of all
people through the millennium. And the more I read
the stronger my imagination grew until I discovered
that I was able to travel into the stories... to actually
become part of them.*

*I wish I could say that I listened to my teacher
and respected my gift, as I ought to have. If I had, I
would not be telling you this tale now.
But I was foolhardy and confused, showing off
with bravery.*

*One afternoon, curious about the myth of the
Arabian Nights, I traveled back to ancient Persia to
see for myself if it was true that every day Shahryar
(Persian: شهريار, "king") married a new virgin, and then
sent yesterday's wife to be beheaded. It was written
and I had read that by the time he met Scheherazade,
the vizier's daughter, he'd killed one thousand
women.*

Something went wrong with my efforts. I arrived in the midst of the story and somehow exchanged places with Scheherazade — a phenomena that had never occurred before and that still to this day, I cannot explain.

Now I am trapped in that ancient past. I have taken on Scheherazade's life and the only way I can protect myself and stay alive is to do what she did to protect herself and stay alive.

Every night the King calls for me and listens as I spin tales. And when the evening ends and dawn breaks, I stop at a point that leaves him breathless and yearning for more. And so the King spares my life for one more day, so that he might hear the rest of my dark tale.

As soon as I finish a story... I begin a new one... like the one that you, dear reader, have before you now.

Prologue

1 year ago…
Pilar

"Your father is dying."

My older brothers and I exchanged a grave look at those words. It wasn't a surprise or a shock. His health had been declining for years, and it was only a matter of time before it happened. None of that made it any easier to prepare for. My mother was stoic even as she laid the news out for us. She once said she'd learned the trait from watching my father. In the silence of his chambers, I tried to form a chant inside my head. "Long live the king!"

It was something people said in pubs while drinking, outside of the palace walls during ceremonies, and in the form of a salute when they met my father. My father. The King of France. The one who was slowly deteriorating in the room next door like many kings before him.

We were well-taught and knew the history of our sovereigns, as well as the ones in my mother's homeland of Spain. The one constant in all of those stories was death. Death by plague, death by combat, death by cancer, but always death. However timely or untimely it may seem. Yet when faced with it, we weren't sure what to do. When confronted by it, we all felt the same thing those outside these walls felt. Even if we didn't show it on our faces like my mother. On the inside, we wept and trembled. We were scared. We felt hollow.

My eldest brother, Elias, took my right hand. My other brother, Aramis, took my left. We squeezed, the three of us knowing that this would change the course of our lives forever. We were the only ones who could possibly understand what the other was feeling, allowed ourselves to wallow as our mother stood with her back to us, her head held high as she looked out the window.

"He wants to crown Elias before he goes," Mother said, her voice shaking. "He wants to be here for that, at least."

Elias's hand tightened on mine. He hung his head as if her words had delivered a blow. I knew they had. One thing Aramis and I did not envy was that Elias was next in line. The idea of being king may seem exciting to some, but we knew the reality of it. The proof was dying in the next room.

"The doctor is giving him six months," Mother continued. "You will all be on your best behavior in the coming weeks. Your father does not want anyone to know about this yet. Not until everything is ready for the coronation. That means you may take your short holiday as you normally do, but no scandals this time. We do not have room for missteps. Elias, you'd do well to use this time to reflect. It may be the last time you're able to do that. Aramis, I beg you to be discreet. Please, no tabloids. Pilar, you've never given us any grief. Please keep it that way."

She turned and faced us. It was then that we saw her grief-stricken expression and bloodshot eyes. The three of us moved closer to each other, huddling in as if to prevent anything from coming between us.

"This is what we've tried to prepare you for your entire lives. Don't let us down."

Chapter One

Pilar

"How hungover are you?" my best friend and personal secretary, Joslyn, asked as she opened all of the blinds.

"Very," I croaked, throwing an arm over my face to shield myself from the sun. "Don't worry, no scandals on my end."

"You sure about that? The chef spotted Benjamin Drake leaving your villa just before five o'clock in the morning."

"What?" I sat up quickly with a gasp. "No."

"Yes." She raised an eyebrow. "I take one night off, and you go out partying without me?"

"I…" I shook my head. "I went to a Hookah bar and then to the club beside it…" I tried to recall memories from last night. "I…yeah, I definitely spoke to Ben. I think we may have danced." I shut my eyes momentarily. "I was extremely drunk."

"And you're on medicine." Joss shot me a heavy stare. "You know better than to mix things like that with alcohol."

"Fuck." I brought my hands to my face and wiped at my eyes. I'd completely forgotten that I'd taken the medicine the doctor had given me for the sinus infection I no longer had. It had been my last day of taking it. "How could I not remember spending the night with Benjamin-bloody-Drake?"

"How indeed?" Joss sighed as she sat on the edge of my bed. "You must have made a good impression though."

"Why do you say that?"

"His people called me an hour ago. He wants you to accompany him to a gala next week."

"Me?"

"Yep."

"Why me? I don't even like public appearances."

Joss had been working as my personal secretary for a short time. So far, hiring her was the best decision I'd ever made. We'd gone to an all-girls college together. Before that, we attended an all-girls high school. We'd known each other since we were born—technically before that since our mothers were pregnant at the same time. As lifelong best friends themselves, they'd proclaimed our friendship fate and were thrilled to see it come to fruition the way it did. I'd be lost without Joss.

That didn't mean I agreed with her about this particular thing. I only made a handful of public appearances because they always resulted in one thing or another. The last event I'd attended on behalf of the Crown had been with my sister-in-law, Adeline, the queen. I'd fallen on my ass walking down a set of stairs. It was morbidly embarrassing to say the least.

Adeline, being the natural that she was, sat beside me and played it off as if we were looking for a lost earring. That was the snap the paparazzi took—two women looking for a family heirloom. It was fine until my mother gave us a lecture on how irresponsible that looked and reminded us how queens and princesses were never meant to be on the floor, etcetera, etcetera.

I looked up and found Joss staring down at her phone with a frown on her face.

"What's wrong?"

"Your brother is an idiot. That's what's wrong."

"Which one?"

"Aramis." She shot me an exasperated look. "He's once again in the headlines. I don't know how Elias is going to handle the stress of the throne and your brother's missteps."

"Who cares?" I yawned. "Aramis has his own secretary to do damage control."

"Ha. You mean the one who quit this morning?"

"What?" I blinked. "George quit?"

"He did indeed." She shook her head, tossing the phone onto the bed. "That makes three secretaries in three weeks. Like I said, he's an idiot."

"Poor George. I liked him."

"Me too." Joss stood up. "Anyway, get up. We have things to talk about and galas to get dresses for."

"What? No. I'm not going to that with Ben. Tell him I'm flattered, but I can't make it."

"You're going to say no to Benjamin Drake? The man you've lusted after for five years? The guy you just spent the night with and can't even remember a single second of?"

"Don't remind me." I reached for the sheet and pulled it over my head. "Tell him I don't make appearances."

"It's for a good cause. It'll be good for the Crown. It'll take the spotlight away from Aramis and in turn, Elias and Adeline, and give them a moment's reprieve."

I'd gotten used to living under a microscope. Sometimes, I absolutely hated it, but I was the sister of the newest King of France. Living under scrutiny was to be expected. My father's passing had garnered all of us even more attention from the press, especially Addie and Elias. The paparazzi loved them, but it had gotten to be too much. They couldn't even walk the Gardens at Versailles without having photos snapped, so I understood when Joss said that this would help to give them a break while they figured things out.

"When is this gala?" I asked, still trying to wrap my head around Benjamin Drake asking me to go with him, and the fact that I'd spent the night with him and didn't remember it.

"Two days."

"Two days?" I sat up in bed. I was wearing my pajamas so I found it difficult to believe Ben and I had done much together. I frowned at that. "Have I heard of the organization?"

"It's the Drake Foundation." She picked up her phone and scrolled on the screen, reading a text or an email. "They open schools and fund after-school activities for underprivileged children."

"So he wants me to go with him to his own foundation's gala?" I asked. "Wasn't he dating an actress?"

"Yes. Sophia Deneuve. They broke things off recently."

"Oh."

Joss walked out of the room, leaving me thinking about Benjamin and Sophia. Was that the kind of woman he liked? I'd run into them together once or twice and always thought they were an odd pair. Not because they weren't gorgeous, but because Ben looked as if he could snap Sophia in half. She was tiny and delicate, and he was rough and muscular with tattoos on seemingly every inch of his perfectly toned body. My face heated. Had I touched his perfect six-pack? The tips of my fingers tingled at the thought. Had I explored his body? Had he explored mine? Oh God. I shut my eyes again and groaned. Leave it to me to spend the night with the most perfect specimen on the planet and not remember a second of it.

Chapter Two

Pilar

I reached up and knocked on the door two times, loudly, and then lowered my hand, wiping my palm on my jeans. I was so nervous. Joss had left earlier, taking a plane back to Paris to deal with the matter of helping Aramis hire a new secretary, leaving me here alone. Well, alone with a handful of guards—one of which was standing nearby. The door opened, and I swore my heart stopped. Seeing Benjamin Drake on television with his shirt off after a game was one thing, but experiencing it in real life? I had no words for this.

He wore shorts that hung low on his hips and a cocky grin on his face that made my heart pump in overdrive. I licked my lips. I was a princess, damn it. I'd met all kinds of people from all different backgrounds. We'd hosted the entire rugby team last year at the palace. We'd had the football team over as well. Still, none of them made me want to rip my clothes off the way Benjamin Drake did.

"Hey." He kept smiling. "What brings you down here?"

"Down here?" I frowned, looking up and down the strip of small cottages.

"Down from your place all the way up on the hill to where the peasants live." He smiled broader as he said the words, and there was nothing condescending about his tone. Still, I felt my frown deepen.

"My villa looks just like yours, and you would know since apparently you spent the night in it. Just so we're clear, I don't remember anything that happened." I felt my face heat but continued. "I was really drunk.

And I'd taken medication because I have a cold I haven't been able to get rid of, so don't let whatever I did or said last night go to your head." I turned around quickly and began walking away.

"Wait." Ben stepped outside and grabbed my arm, turning me toward him, confusion marring his otherwise hard features. "Nothing happened."

"What?"

"Nothing happened between us last night." He let go of my arm and lifted his hand to brush back his unruly curls, letting out a sigh as he dropped his arm again. "I took you home. That was it."

"The chef said he saw you leave at like five this morning." I licked my lips, hating that my face felt so hot when I spoke.

"That's because I managed to get you out of the club at four-thirty." He raised an eyebrow. "Ask your guards. They were there. You didn't want to leave when they asked you to. I facilitated it happening."

"Facilitated how?" I eyed him warily.

"I carried you." His lips spread into a wide, flirty grin. One that I swore would rip me to pieces. I blinked, trying to process what he'd said.

"You carried me out of the club?"

"Yep." He was still smiling.

"Why are there no pictures of that happening?" I eyed him suspiciously, then turned my attention to Amir who stood within earshot. "Is that true?"

"It's true." Amir gave a nod, smiling a little. "No photographers allowed, remember?"

"Right."

It was the reason I'd come here to begin with. I didn't want to go to Marbella like my brothers did every summer. I'd chosen Ibiza because it was an island, and this time of year, even though famous people flocked to it along with big-time DJs, paparazzi were not permitted. At least not on the side of the isle we were on.

"So, I'll see you at the gala?" Ben said.

"Yes, I guess you will." I raised my head and walked away, leaving him looking a little more amused than I cared for.

Ben had attended my mother's famed Sunday dinners a few times, invited by my brothers. Mom welcomed him. Despite that, and the fact that we bumped shoulders often, we hadn't gotten to know each other well. Not really, anyway. Unless you counted the time we were both waiting for our coats while everyone else was outside enjoying the fireworks. We spoke few words, but they were enough to fuel my crush on him. Not that it needed any help. To me, he was a mystery. He showed the world just enough to hypnotize them, but nothing sufficient to let us think we really knew him. In that sense, he was a lot like my family. In every other way, not so much. We weren't far apart in age, but in experience, we may as well have twenty lifetimes between us.

Chapter Three

Ben

I genuinely hadn't been this excited to take a woman out in a long time. I dated plenty. All the time. The tabloids labeled me a playboy, and I took it in stride even though I didn't feel I was a playboy at all. I liked women, I was single, rich, and a hell of a football player. None of those things defined me as a person though. There was more to me that the world didn't know because I made it a point not to show them. I liked the fact that they only saw a smiling, carefree man when they looked at me. It made it less likely for them to dig deeper. So, I dated women who took the limelight off me because they were famous in their own right.

Pilar was the exception though. Not because she wasn't famous. She was a damn princess, but she was never the center of attention. You couldn't find photographs of her doing crazy things. You didn't catch whispers about her or hear rumors. Being seen with Pilar would mean that the paparazzi would eye me a little closer and wonder why she'd leave her sheltered life to step out with me. It was risky, especially since I didn't want them digging. As far as I was concerned, my past and personal life were not up for public debate. My manager had advised against inviting her as my date. My friends counseled against it. My ex, whom I was still close friends with and who stayed out of my business, warned against it.

A part of me knew I should listen to them. A bigger part of me couldn't. Probably the same bit that donned a hard-on every time the princess walked into a room, that I had used to pleasure myself, the image of her riding me hard and fast. The piece I needed to cool the fuck off if I was going to treat her like the royalty she was. Though, even without her title, she would never be some random hookup.

Something about Pilar captivated me. Maybe it was her innocence or the way she carried herself as if she were trying to keep her composure in any given situation. Except last night. Last night, she was wild—dancing on the tables, singing loudly, letting her hair down. A completely different Pilar from the prim and proper one I'd met countless times before. I'd heard from a lot of our mutual connections that she had a crush on me, but she never made it obvious. Every time she saw me, she smiled politely, small-talked, and then moved on to the next person. I hated when she left.

"Everything all right, boss?"

I looked up at David and nodded. My agent had hired David to keep an eye on me when I first came into the league. I was rash back then. Too young, too stupid, and was handed too much money for my own good. It was a careless time for me. Freedom had been given to me quickly, which was another luxury I didn't have back home. And so, the league complained, and my agent got involved and hired David to babysit me.

At first, I was upset. I hated David. He was too prim and proper in his *Gentleman's Quarterly* suits and shiny loafers. A complete contrast to my heavily tattooed body and designer trainers. It took me a year to warm up to him, which was the norm for me. I didn't trust easily. I did everything in my power to push him away, and he just kept coming back. He said the money was too good to give up. Most people laughed, but I knew he wasn't joking. So, David stayed, and I learned to trust him. He taught me that not everyone who comes into your life is looking for ways to destroy it.

"Pilar came by the villa," I said after a while.

"Oh? To accept or decline the invitation?"

"Neither." I shot him a look. "She did accept though."

"I figured she would." He smiled slightly. "She's always had a crush on you."

"She came by because she thought we slept together."

"Why would she think that?" His eyebrows pulled together. "I'm gone a week and you…you didn't, did you?"

"Of course, I didn't. I helped her get home after a night of partying. That's it."

"You said you wouldn't touch her. That was the deal."

"I'm well aware."

"If her brothers find out you hooked up with their baby sister, I don't even want to think about the kinds of things they'll do to the team," David continued. "The only reason you're taking her to the gala is because they know it'll cheer her up. It's been a year since her father's death, and she hasn't gotten back on her feet. One night out with the star of Le Bleus, her crush. But they know you'd never touch her because you're much older, much wiser, and have other women on your mind."

"David, shut the fuck up. I'm not going to sleep with the princess." I sighed, exasperated. "I don't need anyone to remind me of that, and I don't need you babysitting me."

"I know you don't. You know you don't. But you like having me around. I keep you grounded."

"You annoy me."

"Comes with the territory." He shrugged a shoulder, picking up the mimosa he'd been sipping. "Anyway, your tuxedo came in. You should try it on tonight in case you need any last-minute alterations. I'll catch up with you later." He drained his mimosa as he stood and set the empty flute on the table. "I have a date tonight."

With that, he left, leaving me to pay the bill and think about what he'd said. He wasn't wrong. Even though I really wanted Pilar in my bed, there were myriad reasons it shouldn't happen.

The only problem was that I wasn't great at following the rules.

Chapter Four

Pilar

"I feel like my breasts are going to pop out of this dress." I inhaled and held my breath as the designer, Katrina, zipped me up.

"You look gorgeous, honey."

"Your dress is stunning. I look like I'm not supposed to be wearing it." I eyed the form-fitting black gown.

"Nonsense. The minute I finish zipping you up, you'll exhale and see it fits you like a glove."

I didn't want to tell her the glove was too small because I didn't want to offend her, but it sure felt that way. The mere act of breathing made it feel like my ribs would pop out of the dress. When she dropped her hands and stepped back, I exhaled slowly. It was still tight, but...okay.

"Walk around." Katrina waved a hand. "Get comfortable."

"Comfortable?" I wasn't sure that was a word I'd use while wearing this gown, but I started to walk anyway out of fear that Katrina might slap my bottom if I didn't.

She had a grandmotherly air about her, despite being younger than my mother. It was the way her eyes assessed things, not dissimilar to the look I found in Benjamin Drake's eyes when I peered into them. He seemed wise beyond his age, but he was older than my twenty-four years. Of course, I'd met women who were my age and already seemed to have life figured out. Some were married and beginning families. Others were starting careers. I had been coddled for so long, and under such a strict thumb, that I barely knew how to pick out what I wanted to eat at a restaurant when I went out for dinner. It was pathetic, really. It also made me nervous to go out with Benjamin without Joss to take the lead on such matters, but I needed to grow up sometime, and who better than

Benjamin Drake to show me the ropes? I smiled at the thought.

"You love it, don't you?" Katrina said.

"Yes, I do. And it fits perfectly." I faced her with a smile.

"I told you it would." She smiled and nodded once. "Now for the shoes."

"Pilly, we need to—" Joss stopped talking and looked up from her phone as she walked into the room. "Oh my God, that dress is everything on you."

"It's pretty, right?"

"It's perfect." She eyed me up and down. "Ben won't be able to take his eyes off you."

"You think?" I asked, a squeal in my voice as I shimmied my shoulders and looked in the mirror again.

I would absolutely, positively die if Ben put the moves on me. I'd imagined it for so long that I was sure the reality would never live up to the fantasy. But there was only one way to find out.

* * * *

"You look...stunning." Ben's gaze raked over me ever so slowly, making me feel the heat of it over every inch of my body.

"Thank you." I smiled. "You look pretty great yourself."

Great was an understatement for Ben Drake in a tuxedo, but my vocabulary was weak when it came to such matters—which was jarring to me, considering I spoke several languages.

We must have stood there for a full three minutes before he chuckled and looked at the floor. He slowly brought his face up and stared through thick, dark lashes while flashing me a sexy smile. I thought my heart might stop pumping blood right then and there. Wondered if I might die before I went on a formal date with *the* Benjamin Drake. I would die happy though.

"You ready to go?" he asked, seeming amused.

"Yes." I blinked. "Oh my gosh, I don't know what's wrong with me today."

He smiled as if it were no big deal at all as he led me outside. We were flanked by security—both his and mine—and in that instant, I realized that there was no such thing as a normal date. Not for us. I had only been on a few of them, and they'd all been within the palace walls, so

I personally wouldn't count them as dates. Truth be told, I was the youngest twenty-something-year-old ever. Most people my age had lived, *really* lived. I'd only done as much as my parents allowed…which wasn't much. I'd gone to an all-girls boarding school, an all-girls college, and when I got home, my father was dying, which shaved two more years off my life. I wouldn't complain about it though. Not ever. I was a princess and had everything I could ever possibly want, but I didn't have freedom. I didn't have the love of a man. I'd had one boyfriend who was also a virgin when we met, so all of the experiences I'd had with the opposite sex were with someone who was exactly as lost as I was.

"What car are we taking?" I asked, eyeing the three vehicles in front of my villa.

One was my black Range Rover with its heavily tinted windows that Amir rented upon our arrival, another was a white Range Rover I assumed was Ben's, and the third was a shiny Corvette that I also assumed was his. It made my heart skip a beat just thinking about climbing inside.

"We'll take the Corvette." He nodded at our security. "They'll follow behind us."

"Okay." I exhaled shakily and ducked into the car as he opened my door for me. When he sat in the driver's seat, I added, "I hope you're a safe driver."

"Oh, didn't they tell you? I've been pulled over at least ten times for reckless driving." He flashed that smile of his when my eyes widened. "Relax, Princess, I wouldn't put you in peril. I do like my head sitting atop my shoulders." He winked and revved the engine, the car roaring to life. I wasn't sure if the pattering of my heart was from his wink, his smile, or this car, but I liked it.

The event was at a location ten blocks away. During the drive, Ben asked me questions about the happenings in my life (literally nothing at the moment), what I planned to do now that my brother was king (continue to serve the Crown and make more appearances on its behalf), and what I would do if I wasn't a princess (I had absolutely no idea because no one had ever asked me that question). Needless to say, the entire conversation centered around me, and I had no idea how to put the spotlight on him. Finally, when I finished explaining that I had no idea what I would do if I wasn't a princess, I turned to him.

"What would you be doing if you didn't play football?"

"I'd probably be dead. Or in jail." He said it with such ease that it took me a moment to wrap my head around the statement.

"Why?"

"A lot of the guys I grew up with are either dead or in jail." He shrugged a shoulder. "I'd have to assume I'd be one of them."

"That's...intense." I frowned. "What are they in jail for?"

"Drugs. Mostly. A couple are in for homicide."

"Which would you be in for?"

"I'm not sure."

"You're not sure whether or not you would have killed someone by now?" I all but squeaked.

"Things happen, Princess. The real world isn't black and white."

"I know it's not." My frown deepened. "But still. Murder is murder."

"With all due respect, a lot of people consider your father a murderer," he said. "Do you know what the difference is between your father and one of my friends?"

"No, but I'm sure you're about to tell me."

"The crown on his head."

"Right." I looked out the window and thought about that.

Of course, I didn't consider my father a murderer, but there was no use denying the things he'd done when he was alive. Even if I tried to blind myself to his sins, I couldn't hide from the truth—the families affected, the news articles that brought it all to light, etcetera. I wished I could say that I was disturbed by all of it. In a sense, I was. But I was also incredibly embarrassed because he was supposed to be a servant to his subjects, a leader, someone people could go to for help. Instead, they found a person unwilling to yield for the sake of his own traditions. It didn't matter. My father was dead, and my brother Elias wasn't like that. And more importantly, his new wife would never let him become that way. The car slowed and came to a stop in front of the museum where the event was being held.

"Hey, I didn't mean anything by that. I'm just trying to make you see things from another perspective," Ben said.

"I get it. I...thank you." I smiled.

He searched my eyes for a long moment before nodding and getting out of the car to come around and open the door for me. The cameras were on us the second we stepped into view. His hand was around mine, leading me forward, and I focused on that instead of the attention.

Chapter Five

Ben

She was unbelievably nervous, which was something I'd never expected. I'd seen her at galas, at parties, at her mother's Sunday dinners, which were like entering a world summit, with global leaders and famous actors in attendance. She'd never been nervous at those events. It fueled the mystery of Pilar, which wasn't necessarily a good thing since it meant I wanted to see her again. And like David had pointed out to me, sex between us could not happen, and all roads led to sex. I didn't believe that men and women who were attracted to each other could just stay friends, and I couldn't afford to complicate things with the princess. I wanted her for one night, that was it. No strings. Was it a possibility? I wasn't sure, but I'd find out tonight as soon as I got her to loosen up a little.

I let go of her hand when we reached the red carpet they'd rolled out, and she stepped forward to have her photo taken in front of the signs with the logo of my foundation. This would be great press, having her standing in front of those. It would be in all of the tabloids tomorrow morning, which was what I wanted. Not for me, but for what the foundation stood for. I watched Pilar as she smiled, then made a more serious, sexy face and turned to show off the back of her dress. She was a complete natural in front of the camera. All of her previously displayed nerves seemed to vanish when the lights from the flashes hit her. It was baffling. I snapped out of it when David appeared in my line of sight.

"You should step in and have your photo taken with her," he said.

"Yeah." I nodded once and walked over to her.

I'd been staring at her for as long as the photographers had, enthralled by her beauty and poise. I needed to stop idolizing her, thinking of her as some unattainable object. She was a woman, and she was right in front of me. The fact that I knew she had such a huge crush on me was flattering, but now that she was right in front of me, without her brothers or mother or anyone else to stand between us, I wasn't sure what I expected. Perhaps because my conquests had always come easily, I figured she would've flung herself at me already. But she hadn't. Not really, anyway. I didn't count her drunken advances the other night because it would have been unfair to do so. I hadn't told her how she'd slowly stripped down for me and begged me to fuck her. I didn't tell her how difficult it was for me to say no and walk out of there. No. Scratch that. It hadn't been difficult for me to say no because she was out of her mind. If she'd been sober, walking away would have damn near killed me. And now here she was, all innocent again, with that underlying sexiness that I couldn't seem to *not* be attracted to.

I walked over and wrapped an arm around her waist, pulling her to me slightly as the press continued snapping photos of us.

"When did you two meet?" one of the photographers asked. I continued smiling. I wasn't going to give them anything, but Pilar spoke.

"We're old friends," she said. "We both happened to be in town, and I couldn't pass up the opportunity to support this wonderful organization that Benjamin has created."

"Were you familiar with the Drake Foundation before tonight?"

"I knew as much as you did." She winked. "But I know Ben, and when he called me to tell me how the foundation benefits underprivileged children, I knew I wanted to be a part of the unveiling."

"Are you here on behalf of the Crown?" another asked.

"Aren't I always?" Pilar laughed. "But I'm also here because I want to be."

"Are you a couple?" another asked.

I felt Pilar stiffen.

"We'll see you inside," I said, smiling. "Thank you for being here."

I led her away from the photographers. She sighed heavily the second we were out of view. I opened my mouth to say something, but we were interrupted by a man with a silver mohawk and a huge smile directed at Pilar. I kept my hand on her lower back as he introduced himself, first to her and then to me. Bryan Silver.

"Bryan Silver," I repeated. "Fitting. With the hair and all."

"Thanks, mate. I just got it done. My band, Silver Fox, is touring, and I thought it would be a nice touch."

"Silver Fox." I smiled in recognition. His band would be performing here tonight. They were donating any money made to the foundation. I shook his hand again. "Thank you so much for doing this for us."

"Thank you for inviting us. We're massive fans," he said. "*Massive* fans."

"Have you heard them play before?" Pilar asked me.

"I can't say that I have, but I look forward to it."

"They're really great. Good choice, Benjamin." She smiled, the genuine one, and I felt myself grinning back at her.

"Well, I have to finish setting up. I just wanted to introduce myself." Bryan walked away with a slight wave and a wink at Pilar.

I wondered if they'd dated or if he was trying to date her. As far as I knew, not many people had succeeded in taking her out, which was why I'd opted for this event. I knew taking her on a regular date, away from all of the cameras, would have been more ideal, but I also wasn't ready for her to turn me down the way she'd done to so many others.

When I saw her the other night, dancing on tables and drinking her weight in alcohol, she'd opened up and told me how she was supposed to make appearances on behalf of the Crown. In that moment, I thought, *well isn't this an opportunity*? I called my original date and canceled, something I'd have to deal with later. I didn't have any crazy ex-girlfriends, but Kayla wasn't an ex-girlfriend. She was a constant booty call, and she was a little crazy, which was why she remained a booty call and never made it to girlfriend status. And even though I made it clear that going with me to the gala did not mean we were back on in any way, once I canceled on her, I knew Kayla didn't feel that way. It made me even more glad that I'd canceled. It was important to keep a clear line between friendship and something more.

"This is really nice," Pilar said after a moment. I blinked and watched her as she looked at the photographs on the walls.

"It is. Children took these photos," I said.

"What?" Her brows rose as she turned back to look at the rest. "I'm impressed."

The point of this particular exhibition was to raise money to provide art equipment to underprivileged children. The focus of the Drake

Foundation was the kids, but I figured I'd break the events up into parts. This one was about the art, the next would be centered around sports. It was incredible how many children around the world played baseball with a tree branch and a rolled-up sock.

"Where are the kids located? All around the world?" She looked at me briefly before moving on to the next photograph.

"Yes, but the goal is to focus on certain areas at a time. Otherwise, it will get too hectic." I nodded at the next image, a dusty-gray cloud. It looked like just that, a dusty, gray haze, but the reality behind the image was horrifying. "That was taken by a seven-year-old boy in Syria. In the midst of the war. With bombs dropping all around him."

"Oh my God." Pilar gasped, bringing her hand to her mouth. "That's terrible."

"It is, but that's how life is for some people in the world. This serves as a good way to show that."

"It's so sad though." When she turned to me, she looked like she was on the verge of tears. I fought the urge to pull her into my arms. "What happened to the boy?"

"He made it." My smile felt tight. "His parents didn't. His baby sister didn't."

"So sad." She shook her head, turning back to the next photograph.

It was more of the same. Pain disguised as art. Agony wore a lot of masks, but when it was disguised as art, it actually moved people.

"Why Syria?" Pilar turned to me again.

"My brother was a photojournalist. One of his assignments was in Syria during the war. He wasn't welcome there, but he continued to do his job. Despite the treatment, he made friends with some residents, told me great stories about them, about the suffering and sacrifice." I paused, swallowing. I hated talking about this, but she'd asked, and I owed her an explanation.

"My parents didn't approve of this." I signaled toward the photographs. "They said I could have shown the suffering that goes on anywhere in the world. They're bitter about my brother's experience there, but it felt right. We don't get to choose who suffers and who doesn't."

She swallowed visibly and looked at another photograph. "Where are your parents now?"

"Tel Aviv."

"Oh." She raised an eyebrow. "I've never been."

"It's beautiful."

"Is that where you're from? I thought you were from London."

"My father's from London, my mother is from Tel Aviv. I was raised between both places, but my heart was always in Tel Aviv."

"I want to hear more about your family." She smiled up at me.

I chuckled, hoping she'd drop it. A lot was missing from most of my personal stories, and I'd opened up to few people about them. It hadn't bothered my past girlfriends. Kayla was one of the only ones who knew about my parents, and that was only because we'd been hooking up for so many years. Somewhere along the way, the lines had blurred, right before I scrubbed them clean and made it so they'd never blur again. Kayla was what the WAGs, the wives and girlfriends of footballers, called a *hardcore groupie*. When the lines started blurring, it took a sit-down with a few of the spouses for me to realize that she wasn't the woman for me. She'd been sleeping with more than a few of the players on my team behind my back. I probably wouldn't have cared about that as much, had a lot of them not been married. I didn't consider myself above anyone, but their wives were kind, respectful, and much too giving to deserve that kind of treatment. And because I was the one who'd brought Kayla into the mix, I felt guilty. I'd ended things with Kayla, but still kept a casual friendship with her out of habit. Despite being wronged by her, it was difficult for me to completely turn my back on someone I'd known for most of my life.

"I'll tell you about them another time."

"And your brother." Her eyes were filled with questions, but she didn't ask them. It was either because she sensed that I didn't want to speak about any of it, or because she knew it wasn't the place.

She simply smiled again and continued looking at photographs. I wondered how many opinions and questions she kept to herself. I'd seen her in front of her family enough times to know that most of what she did in public was entirely for their benefit. I wished she'd drop the pretense around me. She would. Soon, she would. I just had to prove to her that she could. Though the fact that I wanted to do that at all was a problem in itself.

Chapter Six

Pilar

Everyone loved him. I knew that, obviously, but being out with Ben really made me realize that I was merely one of his many admirers. It was something I should've been used to. It was similar to whenever I went somewhere with Aramis or Elias. Everyone flocked to them—women, men, kids. I was always kind of just there for... I wasn't even sure anymore. At least Ben made me feel like I was *with* him. At his side, not just an accessory he walked around with. He checked in with me, smiled at me from across the room. He winked at me. All things that made me feel as if I couldn't breathe. It was one thing to see him from across the way at one of my mother's Sunday dinners. It was completely different having him here, doing these things purposely. Ben had made it clear that he wanted me. It was crazy, but there was no denying it. He hadn't said it outright, but I knew it just the same. Only I wasn't sure what would happen or how to take things to the next level. Or if he'd even be interested in that. It wasn't like he was the first man to make me feel like he wanted me, but most of them ran for the hills before anything could happen. Most of them were terrified of my family and the scrutiny that came with being seen with a princess.

Everything I knew about Ben told me he was very careful about how he was perceived. Bad boy, fun and easygoing, charming, sexy, those were all adjectives he was familiar and comfortable with. There was a reason for that. Mine were shy, pliant, kind, funny, smart. We all had a role to play, and mine was to make sure people were comfortable.

I'd just finished saying goodbye to someone when Ben walked over to me and put his hand on the small of my back.

"You have a real gift." He started to usher me out of the room and into the hall that led back to the entrance. "If you weren't a princess, you could be an actress."

"Wouldn't that be a dream?" I laughed, turning my head to look at him. As I did, I caught a glimpse of our reflection in the mirror beside us. We stopped walking and stood there. He dropped his hand from my back. "That's what I pretend I am when I'm in front of the cameras. An old Hollywood actress. Like Grace Kelly."

"Much more beautiful than Grace Kelly." He grabbed my hand and lifted it to his lips, kissing the back of my knuckles. Time seemed to slow a bit. I felt myself blush.

"Nobody is more beautiful than Grace Kelly."

He looked at me through the mirror, my hand still in his. He turned me so my back was against his chest and lowered his head, speaking into my ear.

"You are." His eyes were on mine, shades of green and brown muddled together to create the perfect hazel. "The most beautiful."

"You don't have to humor me," I whispered, my chest expanding.

He wasn't even touching me, not really, just holding my hand. Yet it felt like I was completely bare to him.

"I'm not humoring you, Princess. I think about you often. Naked. In my bed. In the shower. Beneath me. On top of me." He lowered his voice, still looking into my eyes, though they were blurring and I could barely keep them open. "But I've been told to stay away. To keep my hands to myself. And I should."

That made me turn swiftly, my steps faltering as I looked up at him. "You shouldn't. Please don't."

"You don't know what you're asking." His voice was hoarse, as if my plea were the ultimate test of his resolve.

"I never ask for anything." I pressed myself closer, my breasts against his chest. "But I'm asking for this."

He brought his face nearer and pressed his lips against mine. In that moment, when everything and everyone around us disappeared, I truly knew what it felt like to be free.

Chapter Seven

Ben

"You shouldn't have kissed her."

"You shouldn't have interrupted me when I was kissing her." I glared at David.

He'd walked into the hall and called out my name at the most inopportune time. I had Pilar against the wall, my lips on hers, one hand on the side of her face, the other cupping her ass, and fucking David had ruined the moment. I'd taken her home and tossed and turned all night, wondering what could have been and giving myself time to just let it be and let her go.

"I'm doing you a favor, Ben. You don't want the media attention this girl will bring."

"What if I do? What if I told you I don't care anymore?"

"Don't you?" He let out a sarcastic laugh. "I know you, and I'm telling you it's a mistake."

Deep down, I knew he was right, but the fact of the matter was that Pilar was four villas down from mine, and I was in my bedroom with a man I did not care to be having a conversation with right now. Especially at this hour. I hadn't even had any coffee yet.

I shot him a look. "Well, then, you did your job. Congratulations. Now if you'll excuse me, I need to get ready for my run."

"Fine. I'll pick you up at three for your press conference." With that, he walked out.

After throwing on a pair of shorts and a T-shirt, I walked out of my room, locked the door behind me, and started running. I wondered what Pilar was up to. Would she still be sleeping? God, what I wouldn't give to sneak into her room and wake her up with my tongue. I shook the thought away and focused on my breathing, trying not to think about the way she felt beneath me. Attempting to keep from summoning the image of what she would look like naked. What it would feel like to bury my cock inside her. My mind was filled with the vision regardless of how hard I tried to push it away. When I stopped for air, I realized I was standing in front of her villa.

Yanking out my earbuds, I let out a heavy exhale, pacing in front of the building. I had no business being here. I was sweating, and the only thing I seemed to want to do was get her sweaty with me. I shut my eyes and pushed my hair off my forehead, still breathing heavily, trying to get myself to just run the last few steps I needed to return to my villa. According to my watch, I'd run six miles up and down the strip, and somehow, I'd still ended up here.

The back door opened. I turned my attention to Pilar, who stood wearing a stringy, powder-blue bikini I could have only thought up in my wildest dreams. Her skin was golden as the sun beamed down, but I could see a milky white triangle from her previous suit, which had covered slightly more than this one. Tan lines weren't something I'd ever fully appreciated until this moment. Now, the only thing I could think about was yanking off her top and exploring her.

Chapter Eight

Pilar

He was simply staring at me. I was peering back and hadn't said a word either, but in my defense, my heart was pounding in my throat, and I didn't know how to make it stop. Ben stood just beneath my balcony, sweaty from a run. Glistening and hot as hell. I'd stood by my window and watched his entire circuit, and when he ended up in front of my villa, I thought I was imagining things. And now that he was standing here, looking my way, his eyes taking in every inch of me, I wasn't sure that I wasn't imagining it. Because it was obvious that he wanted me. Me. Princess Pilar, who nobody ever wanted. Princess Pilar, whom everyone used for personal gain, not for…pleasure.

I took another step forward, letting him see as much of me as he could. He swallowed visibly, but still didn't speak. The only conclusion I could come up with was that he was trying to talk himself out of coming upstairs. Well, I wouldn't let him. I'd have him this once, and then he would be free to leave and regret the whole thing if he wanted to. But I wanted him. Just this once, I wanted something for myself.

"Are you going to come up?" I asked, my voice steady, though my resolve was shaky.

"Are you inviting me?"

"You didn't strike me as a man who waited for an invitation."

My response seemed to crumble whatever barrier he was trying to keep up, because the moment I spoke the words, his expression darkened, and he stepped up to the villa. I couldn't see him below, but I heard his voice and those of the guards. They knew to let him up. I'd already told them that he had clearance to enter whenever he wanted. Of course, I'd thought that might have been last night after he kissed me silly and dropped me off at home. But he hadn't come over. I'd spent the entire night tossing and turning, imagining him sneaking in and having his way with me. The only thing that had happened was that I woke, alone, bathed in sweat in response to the sex-crazed dream I had of him. Not even Joss had been here. She'd been summoned back to Paris to deal with my brother's bullshit, and I was left with a handful of guards, a hot football player, and a heart that felt the need to beat out of control every time Ben was around.

By the time he reached the top of the stairs, I was the one out of breath and sweating. He wasted no time pulling off his sweaty T-shirt and wiping his face with it. As sexy as he looked, my nose wrinkled.

"What's wrong, Princess?" He grinned slowly, that panty-dropping smile that no doubt got him anything he wanted. "You want me to be clean before we get to the dirty part?"

"I…I don't know." I licked my lips. How did he manage to make me feel this way with just a few simple words?

"Do you want to join me in the shower?" He walked toward the bathroom as if he owned the place.

It was off-putting, albeit kind of hot. No one did this around me. I found myself trailing behind him, my gaze glued to his body as he discarded more items of clothing—trainers, socks, running shorts. I held my breath. His underwear would be next. He glanced at me over one broad, dark shoulder.

"Enjoying the show?"

"I can't say that I'm not." I licked my lips again.

"Good." He smiled as he hooked his fingers in the waistband of his boxers and dragged them down, ever so slowly.

His body was a work of art. I'd known that before this striptease, but as I bit my lip hard to keep from making any noise that would change the course of this moment, I knew it to be true. Benjamin Drake had the best body I'd ever imagined on a man. He stepped into the shower and switched on the water. He was no longer watching me, but I couldn't take my eyes off him. I hadn't even looked…*there* yet. I didn't know why. It wasn't like I hadn't seen a cock before. It had only been one before this, but I wouldn't dwell on that. How different could cocks be anyway?

My feet moved toward the glass. Ben was in the middle of soaping himself when his attention snapped to me. I placed my hand on the glass, hoping the steam wouldn't block my view of him. He was no longer smiling. His expression was lustful and dark as he watched me watching him. Every single nuance I'd dreamed of seeing on his face was directed at me. Slowly, he dragged one hand over his ripped muscles as he massaged soap in between his legs. My gaze finally fell there. My chest expanded on a gasp as I took him in, realizing that all cocks were *not* the same. Toby, my ex-boyfriend, had not been this big.

Ben closed a fist around his girth and let out a growl that had me biting my lip. Before I could fully comprehend what I was doing, the hand that wasn't on the glass was on my breast, pinching my nipple through the thin fabric. Then, the other was suddenly on my stomach, dipping under my bikini bottom. Ben groaned louder. My hands moved faster—one sneaking beneath the triangle top to fully cup my breast, and the other making small circles over my clit, to the tempo of Ben pleasuring himself.

"You're wrecking me, Princess." His voice was gruff. "I'm trying not to pull you in here and lift you up to fuck you against the wall."

"I want you to." I was panting now. "Please fuck me against the wall."

"You're impossible." He growled, throwing his head back as he pumped faster. "Fuck. I have never wanted anyone as much as I want you."

"Then have me." I stopped touching myself and pulled the shower door open. The steam smacked me in the face. "Have me."

Ben's erection was now visibly throbbing in his tight grip, and I had never in my life wanted to be on my knees as much as I did in that moment. Instead of saying it, instead of tiptoeing around it, I stepped into the stall and dropped down, my hand replacing his as I licked him. He let go and threaded his fingers into my hair, pulling me back slightly so that my lips weren't touching him. I glanced up at him, the water spraying over my head making it difficult to stop blinking.

"Have you ever been on your knees, Princess?"

"No." I shook my head slightly.

I wasn't going to lie for brownie points. I had no idea what I was doing, and I was okay with that because I'd watched plenty of videos on the matter. His grip tightened on my hair. I yelped, and he let go a bit, but not much.

"Have you ever taken a cock into your mouth before?"

"No." My voice came out shaky.

"Hell." He shut his eyes tightly and then took a deep breath, his abs contracting beautifully. I brought up a hand to trace them. He opened his eyes and looked at me when he felt my hand on him. "I'm not sexist. I'm about as equal opportunity as they come, but having you on your knees before me and knowing I'm your first drives me fucking crazy. Tell me I'm wrong to be glad to be the only one." He pulled me to him again.

I opened my mouth and caught the tip of his cock between my lips. I licked, not slowly as I had before, but like a starving woman who couldn't get enough. Between his tight grip and his rock-hard cock, I really couldn't get enough. I felt as if I would die if he didn't let me pleasure him like this. I brought both hands to him and used them to help me keep him inside my mouth, to suck, to lick wildly. He chanted my name, *"Pilar, Pilar, Pilar."* It was so much better than *Princess*. It was better than anything I'd ever heard in my life.

When he yanked me off him, it was only to stand me up and kiss me on the mouth, his lips crashing over mine in a frenzy—hard and fast and punishing. He was acting irrationally, slightly insane, and his words from before came back to me. He said he'd never wanted anyone this much. I believed him. I couldn't imagine him acting this way—ever. Not Benjamin Drake, the footwork god on the turf, the unattainable playboy of the tabloids, the charming, well-spoken man at my mother's Sunday dinners. He was an array of things, and none of them could have prepared me for the sexual beast before me.

I kissed him with reverence because every moment I'd tried to picture this had paled in comparison to the reality. His hands were rough but worshiping as they explored my curves, cupped my breasts. When he broke the kiss, it was to yank the triangle bikini top off me so he could kiss and lick my chest, biting a nipple a bit roughly. I felt something pool between my legs, and heard myself cry out when he repeated the motion on my other breast. My nails dug into his shoulder blades.

"Ben," I whispered.

He ignored me, dragging his mouth lower, kissing and licking and biting every inch he could until he got to my bikini bottom and yanked it off as well, throwing it against the glass and letting it fall with a loud splat. His tongue swiped between my legs, and my knees buckled in an instant. His grip tightened on my butt as he looked up and met my hazy gaze.

"Tell me, Princess, has another man ever done this to you?"

"One other." My voice was shaky. "But…not like this."

"Not like this." He brought his tongue to me again, licking once, twice, three times. I moaned and brought my hands to his hair, gripping the strands the way he'd done with mine. I felt like I might pass out, stars flying before my eyes as his tongue worked its magic.

"Please, Ben. I can't take it. I can't—"

His mouth moved again, not stopping this time. He was feasting on me, his mouth unlike anything I'd ever experienced or imagined. I gasped, holding onto his hair, pressing my back against the wet tile behind me, unsure of what to do and how to stay upright as the tingly sensation spread through me and then exploded. I moved against his mouth, unwilling to let it end, ever. He didn't stop. He didn't pause. He just kept licking and sucking and moaning against me as if what he was doing brought him great pleasure. When I said his name three more times, he finally stopped, lifted me up in his arms as if I were as light as a feather, before pushing me against the tile and pressing against me to hold me up as he brought his mouth to me again.

"I can't take anymore, Ben. I can't." I was crying, panting, out of breath. He positioned himself between my legs.

"I'll need a condom," he said.

"Are you…?" I paused. I couldn't believe I was asking this. "Are you clean?"

"I am, but we need a condom."

"I'm on the pill."

"We still need a condom, Princess." He kissed my jaw and then bit it before dragging his lips to my neck.

One of his hands found its way between my legs, his fingers on my clit teasing before he put them inside of me. He began pumping as if he were fucking me. With his other hand, he stroked himself, somehow managing to keep me aloft and against the wall. His eyes were on mine, and I couldn't look away. He was pleasuring us both against the wall of a shower. I exploded around his fingers quickly. I couldn't even last a minute. I managed to climb off him and set my feet on the floor, replacing his hands with mine. I stroked him hard, with the same intensity that he had been with himself. I kneeled before him, stroking more, then brought my mouth to him again.

"I'll come, Princess. I'll come…" His words were choppy. "I'll come...oh fuck, I'm going to...I'm going to...take your mouth away. I'll come in your..."

And then he did.

He exploded into my mouth, and all of the tangy, thick substance went everywhere—down my throat as I tried to swallow it, on my lips as I moved back, because even though I had known it would happen, it was still unexpected for it to happen like that. I felt him everywhere. And when we both came back to reality, we washed it all away.

Chapter Nine

Ben

Never hook up with a princess.

We hadn't even actually fucked, yet everyone who came before her suddenly became faceless, and I didn't want to think about anyone coming after either. I was cautious as to who I let into my life. David had warned me not to get in too deep with Pilar, and now that I'd gotten a taste, I was fucked. Literally and figuratively.

"That was…" Pilar licked her lips, a bright blush on her face as she looked down at the floor.

"Legendary."

"Yes." She looked at me, laughing lightly. "Legendary."

She had put on another bikini with a mesh coverup. And I now wore a white robe. I figured I could walk back to my villa dressed in it, and people would only think I was at the spa. No paparazzi were allowed on this part of the island. They had been given strict orders not to bother us, as this was one of the only places in the world we could come to pretend everything was normal. Nobody else here would judge. We were all doing the same things, after all.

"I have a meeting in a bit." I stood up and walked over to her. She was biting her lip, looking down again. I lifted her chin so she could look at me. "That was the most amazing experience of my life."

"You're just saying that." She tried to move, to look away, but I kept her head in place.

"I would never just say that. I don't have to pretend. With anyone." I kissed her. It was meant to be a quick peck, but it deepened quickly. I walked forward, she stepped back, crashing into the dresser behind her. My cock was already getting hard again. "I want you."

"I don't have condoms," she whispered against my lips.

"I'll buy some."

"And then you'll come back?"

"Are you inviting me to lick you again, Your Highness?"

"Don't call me that," she whispered.

"Why not?" I brought my hand to her thigh, lifting up the dress thing she wore and stopping at her bottoms. "It makes you wet."

"It does not."

"No?" I moved my fingers and slid them into her suit. She was so fucking wet. "Princess?"

She moved, pressing herself against me. "Just do it."

"Do what?"

"Put your fingers inside me."

"Because you're wet, Your Highness?"

"Oh my…God!" She screamed when I put my fingers inside her and used my thumb on her clit. She was so fucking sensitive, this woman. It was the ultimate turn on. It was everything I knew she'd be. But fuck, the reality was so much hotter. She let her head fall back, leaving her neck exposed. I licked her there while my fingers worked her. She was close. I knew she was. She panted my name.

"Ben. I'm going to…" she said. "I really want you to fuck me. Please. We're both clean."

It was a hard no, me fucking anyone without a condom. I trusted her. I believed her when she said that she was on the pill and clean, but I couldn't do it. No matter how much I wanted to. I just couldn't. I wouldn't. She was gasping for air, begging for my cock as she found release. I waited for her to come down from the orgasm before stepping away fully and looking at her. She was the most beautiful woman I'd ever seen. I kissed the tip of her nose.

"I'll be back later. With condoms," I promised.

"I can't wait." She smiled. A real one. A shy expression.

The best kind in the world.

With that, I turned and left. I walked to my villa, phone in one hand, dirty clothes in the other when I looked up and spotted David with his arms crossed.

"You fucked her, didn't you?"

"I used her shower is all."

"What's wrong with yours?" He followed behind me as I walked into the villa, tossing the dirty clothes by the laundry room as I passed.

"I'm not sure. Haven't used it today."

"You wanker. I told you not to fuck her. I told you not to—"

"I know what you said." I put up a hand. "Pilar is a grown woman. She makes her own choices, and she happened to approach me about this."

"Did she? So you have an arrangement now? You signed a non-disclosure agreement with the Crown?"

"No." I frowned. "They don't make you sign an NDA."

"This is a mistake, Ben."

"So you've said." I took off the robe and started to get dressed for my interview. "I'm telling you, it's fine."

"Okay. If this blows up in your face, I'm not going to help do damage control."

"Yes, you are." I winked at him. "I pay you too much for you *not* to do damage control."

"Wanker." He walked out of the room, shaking his head. A second later, he called out, "Ring your mother. She's been calling."

I sighed heavily. I loved my mom to pieces, but she was the last person I wanted to call after having mind-blowing oral sex, and David knew that. Asshole.

Chapter Ten

Pilar

"I don't want to get ahead of myself here, but it was the best sex—albeit oral and with hands—of my entire life," I said.

"And it was with Benjamin Drake." My sister-in-law Adeline was quieter than usual, and I couldn't tell if it was because she was in front of people, jealous, or shocked. She was married to my brother, newly married at that, and completely in love, so I put a strike through jealous immediately.

"You're too quiet," I said finally.

"I'm trying to process this," she said. "I thought you told me you'd only had sex with one guy. And this wasn't even full-on sex."

"That's hardly the point."

"It's just…Ben has a reputation. Not that I have to tell you that, but it's something to keep in mind."

"I know."

"He's not exactly a relationship kind of guy. And I mean, what do we really know about him? Aside from him being hot and an amazing football player?"

"Not much." I bit my lip, wishing the concern in her voice wasn't turning into worry in my head. "My mother does background checks on everyone who goes to Sunday dinner. She has dossiers and stuff, but only you guys have access to that."

"You want me to break into the files and see what I can find on him?" Addie asked, sounding as if it were the last thing in the world she wanted to do.

"Yes."

"Well, you'll have to give me a few days," she said after a long pause. "Eli is really stressed right now, and I don't want him mad at me over this."

"I don't want Eli involved at all. But I guess if you must tell him, it's fine. I don't want you fighting over me."

"In that case, I'll get back to you by tomorrow." I could hear the smile in her voice, and it made *me* smile.

"Thank you, Addie. You're the best of the best."

"Hey, the way I see it, if this all works out, there's a chance Benjamin Drake may be my future brother-in-law. I consider this a win for all."

"Don't get ahead of yourself. You said it yourself, he doesn't seem like the relationship type." I laughed weakly. "Besides, I can't be the girl who gets attached to the first rebound she has mind-blowing almost-sex with."

"I don't think sex and love work that way," Adeline said softly. "Love you. Have fun, and I'll get back to you with any important information I find on him."

"Thanks again, Addie."

"Talk to you soon."

I tossed the phone onto my bed and lay back with a heavy sigh. Joslyn would definitely find dirt on Ben fast if I asked her to, but she was so busy right now. I wasn't sure I wanted to bring it up to her until later. Besides, she wasn't here, which meant I didn't have to tell her every single thing that was happening in my life right now. I grabbed my bag and decided to head to the market. Maybe I'd get a few items for tonight. Like wine and cheese and stuff that I probably already had in the kitchen but wanted to buy again anyway because I was bored and needed a distraction.

I was always flanked by security. It was something I never really even thought about until I was out in public, and my guards garnered attention. When people stopped and stared or snapped pictures on their phones as we walked by, that was when I remembered that my security was there to do just that—secure and protect. It had never come to that. Not with me anyway. People saw me, snapped their photos. When I was in France, they occasionally shouted something nice to make me smile. When I was out of the country, people rarely knew who I was right off the bat. Most of them had to use the photo they took to later investigate. I had never been interested in celebrity status. Like everything else, it came with the territory. And like most things, I'd give a lot to live life without it for a day.

"Are you planning on grabbing lunch while we're here?" The question came from Amir, my right-hand guard. I smiled.

"You only ask me that when you're hungry."

"I'm always hungry." His lips moved just a touch, enough for me to know he was smiling without breaking his scary bodyguard persona.

"Let's stop then. I assume you already looked up all of the restaurants in the area and know their ratings." It was something Amir did that we all poked fun of him for. God forbid we eat a meal somewhere rated under four stars.

"There's an Indian restaurant up ahead that's good." He nodded toward a building in the corner. "We could eat Spanish food if you prefer, but that's all you've been eating since we got here, and I'm a little tired of it."

"Indian is fine." I smiled.

We headed in that direction. As we reached the door, a woman came up to us. I smiled, my usual friendly expression in place as she approached. It faltered when I saw the anger in her eyes. I stopped to fully assess her. Amir took up a stance that made it clear I was not to be touched. The woman, who was probably only a little older than I was, looked at him for a second before training her eyes on me.

"You should walk away from Ben before you get hurt."

"Wh…what?" I felt myself frown momentarily until it occurred to me that she was probably a fan and had seen photos of him and me together. I offered her another small smile. "Oh. He's just a friend."

"Ben doesn't keep women friends."

"We're going to have to ask you to step away from the princess." Amir lifted an arm across my chest.

"It's okay, Amir." I looked back at the woman.

"Just be warned. You'll never be the most important woman in his life. I should know. I was there before you, and I'll be there after you." This time, she smiled at me. "I'm the only one he travels with. Which means, I'm always there for him. Waiting. And even I'm not enough for him. Just remember that the next time he leaves your villa."

She gave a little wave, and the phone in her hand lit up long enough for me to see that her lock screen was set on a picture of her and Ben. I watched as she walked away, my heart in my throat, wondering if the things she'd said were real. It wasn't as if I knew all of the women Ben had dated, but I'd stalked him on social media and followed the gossip columns he'd been featured in long enough to recognize most of the women he'd been out with. If she was one of them, I'd remember.

She was beautiful, in a 1960s Italian actress way, with full hips, plump lips and big, brown eyes that glimmered when she smiled. I couldn't help picturing her with Ben. They matched the way couples who have been together for decades did. I imagined his dark complexion against hers, fantasized what their kids would look like if they had any—adorable little curly-haired, plump-lipped babies. I shook the thought away and made myself stop obsessing about it. I hated that my brain conjured images in the blink of an eye. Still, now I couldn't un-see any of it, and I wasn't sure what to think about what had happened between Ben and me. Had he done those things to me and then gone to her to finish the deed? The thought made me feel inadequate.

"Do you want us to follow her?" Amir asked.

"No." I swallowed and turned back to the door. "We don't follow people anymore."

There was no use mentioning that I already had Adeline looking into Ben's file. Those were matters best left within the family, and even though I cared about Amir as if he *were* part of my family, at the end of the day, this was a job for him. I didn't want more drama for my brother, not when he was doing everything in his power to start a clean reign, where people trusted him to make decisions that were best for them. I sat down with Amir at a table by the window, wishing that Joss were here for me to talk this through with. She was a woman and had more experience than I did with matters like these. Instead, I was stuck with my bodyguard, who, despite his fitness regimen and style, could be my father.

"I have a question," I said after the longest silence ever.

"About the woman?"

"No." I shot him a look. "I already told you to leave that alone."

"What's your question?" He ripped off a piece of paratha and dipped it into the chickpeas, scooping it up swiftly. He watched me as he chewed. I tried to think of a way to ask my question that didn't seem lame, but Amir knew me, so it really wouldn't matter.

"Let's say you really like a person who's famous—" I started.

"Like you." He waved another piece of paratha at me.

"No. Not like me. I mean really famous."

"You're pretty famous."

"No, I'm not. My brothers are. I'm just the princess who lives in their shadows."

"That's not true." He frowned. His thick, dark eyebrows made him look menacing to others when he did this, but it always made me smile because Amir was the biggest sweetheart. "What's your question?"

"My question." I took a deep breath. "So, let's say you really like a professional athlete, a really famous one, and he or she finally asked you out—"

"She," he said.

"For the love of God, Amir, stop getting tripped up on the details."

"Okay." He chuckled. "Continue."

"So, she or he asks you out, and you have the best time. Then, you see each other again, and have an even better time. Only this person just so happens to be friends with your brothers—"

"Let's pause there," Amir said. "I feel like this is an important detail since your brothers will likely kill him when they find out."

"Well, then, it's a good thing they're not going to find out. And it's another good thing they don't have a reason to kill him." I flashed my please-shut-up-now smile at him, and he continued eating. "So, you really like this person, but you're fully aware that you don't know much about them. Do you continue seeing them and start asking real questions to get to know them, or do you just enjoy your time and have fun and take it for what it is?"

"What is it?"

"What is what?"

"You said take it for what it is. What *is* it?"

"Oh." I frowned. "I don't know."

"Maybe you should find out before you decide whether or not to ask more questions or lay off."

"I guess."

"Benjamin Drake seems like a good guy, despite all of the tabloid rumors about him being a playboy."

"Oh my God, Amir. This is all hypothetical!"

"Sure. Maybe it can be hypothetical with someone who's not with you twenty-four-seven." He smiled. "Don't worry, I've been sworn to secrecy."

I groaned and shook my head. Amir *had* been sworn to secrecy, but so had all of the other guards and house workers, and they loved to gossip more than the rags. I could already hear the whispers, and they hadn't even started. Part of me was amused by it. The other part wished I could call a house meeting and get all of their takes on the matter. Because I honestly had no idea what I was doing. Men were kind of a mystery to me, but Ben Drake was completely uncharted waters.

Chapter Eleven

Pilar

I looked at the tabloid headline again.

"Princess Pilar Following in Brothers' Footsteps."

It was accompanied by a photograph of me in my bikini and barely there coverup on my balcony. It must have been taken right after Ben had left because it was clear as day that I'd just gotten screwed. Literally and figuratively, apparently.

"I thought paparazzi weren't allowed on this part of the island." I looked up at Amir.

"Which means, it wasn't a paparazzo who took this."

"This is so embarrassing." I covered my face. "What will Eli say?"

"I spoke to him. He doesn't want you to worry."

"I look…" I dropped my hand from my face and peered at the grainy photograph of myself. At least it was grainy. Still, you could make out my expression. "I look like a porn star."

Amir flinched. "Please don't say that."

"I'm just saying what everyone else is probably thinking." I set the magazine down with a sigh. "I know Aramis won't yell at me for this because that would be hypocritical, but Eli? I don't even want to face him."

"I already told you, I spoke to him. He doesn't seem upset. He wants you to have fun, you know?"

"Having fun is one thing, but at what cost to the Crown?"

"You having fun or doing things like this is perfectly normal, Pilar.

You're twenty-four not eighty-five. And quite frankly, you've never stepped out of line. This hardly constitutes something you should be ashamed of. It's not like you're spitting in babies' faces."

I felt myself laugh. "Well, you're the most by-the-book person I know, so I guess if you're not judging me, I should calm down."

"Exactly."

"I just don't understand. Who would take this photo and sell it?"

"Who knows." He shrugged. "We're going to make sure it doesn't happen again though."

Amir walked away like a man on a mission, and I was sure he'd make good on that promise. My mind went back to the woman I'd met outside of the Indian restaurant. Could it have been her? I shook my head. No. I doubted it. People who took photographs like these and sold them were usually in the gossip mill industry. I decided to let it go. It was the only thing I could do right now. I stood, tossed the tabloid into the trash, and went to my room to call Joss. She was my personal secretary and in charge of keeping gossip at a minimum. If anyone would know what to do right now, it was her.

* * * *

I stared at the vase of red carnations.

"These were sent to me?" I asked for the second time.

Nobody had sent me flowers before. I hadn't even read the note yet, but I knew who they were from. I just couldn't process how I felt about it.

"Yes, Miss Pilar," said Sylvia, our cleaning lady. I'd told the staff not to address me formally, but they couldn't seem to stop doing it, so I accepted the *Miss*. Sylvia cleared her throat. "Red carnations mean longing. Did you know that?"

"I didn't." My heart pounded as I walked up to the vase and picked up the envelope, opening it and taking out the little card.

We didn't exchange phone numbers. Can we see each other again? Tonight? –
Ben

He'd included his number on the bottom of the card. I felt myself smile as I read it over and bit my lip as I took out my phone to type in his number. I didn't mean to call, but I pressed the button instead of saving the digits. He answered quickly, sounding a little out of breath. My breath caught at the sound of his pants. I instantly thought about the woman I'd met on the street and wished that wasn't my first thought when it came to his heavy breathing.

"Pilar?"

"Yes, it's me."

"You got the flowers." I could hear the smile in his voice.

"I did. I guess the note answers the first question that came to mind when I saw them."

"What question was that?"

"I don't know. I just… I guess I didn't expect flowers." I bit my lip. "But you didn't really have my number to text me."

"Text you?" he said. "You think I sent flowers in lieu of a text because I didn't have your number?"

"Well, didn't you?"

"No, Pilar." He was quiet for a second. "Boys send texts. Men send flowers."

"Oh." Happiness flooded me. "Do you send flowers to all the women you hook up with?"

"Not all."

"Hmm. Only the ones you want to see again?"

"Pretty much."

"Well, thank you for your honesty." I laughed lightly. "For a minute there, I thought you were going to tell me you'd never sent anyone flowers before."

"I don't need to use lies to impress you. I'd rather do that with actions."

"I like that." I smiled. "So, tonight? At nine? Ten? I want to do something fun."

"In that case, I'll pick you up at ten. Wear something comfortable. Nothing too fancy."

"See you then." I hung up the phone and let out an excited shriek.

"I take that as a good sign," Amir said, walking into the dining area. He approached the flowers. "Carnations. Interesting. Most men send roses."

"Carnations signify longing." I jutted my chin proudly. "Sylvia just told me that."

"Longing is a good sign." Amir smiled. "So, tonight at ten?"

"Do you just sit around eavesdropping on all of my conversations?"

"Not all of them. Only the ones you have in public areas of the house."

I stared at him for a long time before walking away and into my room to pick out an outfit for tonight. I would compare Amir to my father, but if I were being completely honest, Amir was more of a father to me than my own. I had been sad when Father died because when everything was said and done, he was still my dad, but honestly, I was sadder at the thought of losing someone like Amir. After a few minutes, there was a knock on my door.

"Come in," I called out, knowing it was Amir again.

"Joss is coming in tomorrow for a few days. She said she tried calling but couldn't reach you. I told her your reception wasn't good in most of the house."

"Thank you." I glanced at him with a smile before going back to the clothes in front of me. "Do you think casual, not fancy, means like a maxi dress?"

"What is a maxi dress?"

"This." I pulled one out and pressed it to my front.

"That's nice." He nodded. "You should wear a coverup over it though."

"A coverup?" I laughed. "It's hot. The whole point of this is to feel sexy."

"Well, in that case, don't wear a coverup." He kept staring at the dress like he wanted to say something but wasn't sure if he should. Finally, I sighed.

"What?"

"You should take it slow with Benjamin."

"You said he was a good guy."

"Even good guys hurt good people unwillingly."

"You think he's going to hurt me?" I lowered the dress with a frown.

"Not willingly, but you're very innocent for your age, Pilar. You've been sheltered a lot."

"I've done things." My frown deepened. I had.

"You've had one long-term boyfriend who you were with for nearly six years. That doesn't give you room to do a lot of things."

"Yeah, well, Toby and I—"

"Grew up together." Amir smiled. "And that's a wonderful thing. He loves you very much."

"I'm not getting back together with Toby."

"It's not my place to suggest you should."

"Good. So we're clear on that."

"We are. See you in a while. I have to go run some errands before tonight."

"He said he's picking me up," I called out.

"Sure, which means we have to do what we did last time and trail you around. Nothing says 'we're going on a regular date' like a caravan full of security surrounding an overzealous sports car."

I laughed at his tone as he walked away and closed the door, but as time went on, I thought about what he'd said, and it dawned on me that being with the same guy for six years essentially meant that I was innocent in matters of love. I wasn't sure how I felt about that.

Chapter Twelve

Pilar

I'd been thinking about whether or not to bring up the photograph to Ben. I decided against it. Firstly, I didn't want to call attention to it if he hadn't seen it. And secondly, I decided that I didn't care. Maybe a local had taken the picture to sell for money they needed to feed their family. It wasn't like I was naked. I was over it.

The doorbell rang, and even though I had been pacing the area in front of it for the last ten minutes, I stopped and just stared at it for a second. I couldn't have him thinking I was waiting around for him. After counting to ten, I took a deep breath and walked over, unlocking and opening the door. Ben stood on the other side, wearing ripped jeans and a black T-shirt that clung to him. His dark, curly hair looked as if he'd just run his hands through it just before leaving the house, and it only added to his sex appeal.

"You look beautiful." He smiled, eyes twinkling. "I told you to dress casual because I figured we could have a quiet dinner in my villa, but you're making me want to take you out."

"You can take me anywhere." It took all of half a second for me to laugh at my overeagerness. Ben merely grinned. I licked my lips and tried again, "I mean, I don't care where we go."

"Let's go to a club and see where the night takes us." He winked. Butterflies took flight inside me.

"Okay." I glanced behind me and found Amir standing a few feet away, looking at his phone. He glanced up when he felt my attention.

"Ready?"

"Ready," Ben confirmed.

I followed him outside and stopped as he opened the passenger door, waiting for me to settle into the low seat before closing me in and walking to the other side of the vehicle. I watched as Amir climbed into the driver's seat of the SUV parked in front of Ben's car. Ben got into the driver's seat and typed something quickly on his phone.

"Amir wants me to give him our full itinerary. I guess flying by the seat of our pants won't work with you." He shot me a sideways glance and a sexy smile.

I wanted to tell him to forget Amir but knew that was an impossible task. The island was too small, and he'd find us in two seconds. Besides, even though I was here to escape the scrutiny and live my life for once, I couldn't seem to shake the responsibility resting on my shoulders that came with my title and my brother being the king. Instead, I stayed quiet. I was good at that. He was quiet too, and I wondered if it had anything to do with the woman who'd confronted me earlier today. I opened my mouth to tell him about her but quickly shut it again. He should open up to me about her. Or not. It was like Amir had suggested, Ben didn't seem to do serious relationships. If I wanted him in any capacity, I needed to keep that in mind.

He pulled up in front of the club where I'd seen him my first night here. I could hear the music blasting from inside, and we were still in the car with the windows up.

"This place?" I looked over at him.

"You didn't like it?"

"I did." I bit my lip. "But I also made a lot of bad decisions that night."

"Well, I won't let you make too many tonight. But if you do, I'm here to make sure nobody takes advantage of you." He winked. I bit my lip harder, feeling myself blush. Ben chuckled. "What?"

"What if I want to be taken advantage of?"

"Then I would say it depends. If you mean by some random guy in there"—he raised an eyebrow, pointing toward the nightclub—"I'd say you're out of luck because I'm not going to let that happen. If you're insinuating what I think you are, I'm here for it."

"Good." I was still blushing, but I smiled. "Shall we, then?"

Before he got a chance to come around to open my door, Amir was there, opening it and helping me out of the car.

"Are you sure you want to be at this place?"

"Why not? I'm here to have fun."

"There are two famous DJs in here tonight. It'll be crowded. I called the manager from the car and was able to secure a hidden area in the VIP section." Amir's expression was serious. "As long as you know what you're getting yourself into."

"I'll be fine." I smiled and looked at Ben, who was coming around the car.

I wasn't sure what I expected him to do, but reaching for my hand was not one of the options. So, when he did, a thrill ran through me. We followed Amir as three other security detail members surrounded us. Even though the paparazzi weren't allowed here, it didn't surprise me that people with phones pointed them at us, snapping photos and taking videos as we passed. I looked at Ben to see how he was reacting to it. If his head was down, I'd keep mine down as well, but he held his high, his smile prideful, his hand tightening around mine. I smiled widely, unable to contain my excitement, and looked forward with my head held high as well. I was happy to be here with him, and I had absolutely nothing to hide. We were escorted upstairs to a dark, secluded area, right above the DJ. Ben kept my hand in his as he spoke to the waitress, and I looked around. He tugged my hand and led me to the couch, where we still had a view of the stage the DJ was on.

"What do you want to drink?" He brought his mouth near my ear.

"Anything," I shouted. "Vodka?"

"I got vodka and tequila." He smiled. "I don't think I've ever seen you drinking. I mean, last time excluded."

"I don't normally." I laughed. "You know my family."

"I do, and they party pretty hard." He looked amused.

"I was never allowed to do that. This is my vacation from them, and the first time I'm experiencing all of this." I frowned, meeting his eyes. "I've been to clubs, it's not that I haven't, but I don't actually... I don't know. I don't know how to explain it."

"You don't let yourself go."

"I guess," I said after a moment of mulling it over. "But last time I went overboard. I was also on some medication I'd forgotten about."

"Medication for what?"

"I had a sinus infection, and they gave me meds for it. It was my last day on them, but they must have been pretty hardcore because I blacked out."

"I won't let you do that today."

I smiled and watched as the waitress set our bottles on the table and then put out glasses for us.

"That's a lot of alcohol," I said.

"I have friends passing by. I hope that's okay."

"Yeah, of course." I smiled. "Do you introduce everyone to your friends?"

"Not everyone." He smiled as he reached for the bottle of vodka and poured it into our glasses. "Juice or soda?"

"Juice, please."

"I only introduce important people to my friends and family."

"Important people," I echoed. "And I'm on that list?"

"It appears so."

"So…" I sighed. "I feel like I should tell you something."

"Sounds serious." He sat back on the couch after handing me my glass and taking a sip from his own. "What's up?"

"A woman approached me this morning on my way to lunch. She said a lot of things I can't even remember right now, but at the end of it, she suggested that you always travel with her. That she's the one you always go back to."

"Kayla." He exhaled heavily, shaking his head. "What did she say?"

"I honestly don't remember. My mind was racing, and I couldn't focus on all of it. Something about you having a woman you put in front of everyone, but I don't know if she meant her or someone else." I bit my lip and took a hefty gulp of the vodka and orange juice, trying not to cringe when I swallowed. First drinks were always the hardest. "And then I realized I don't know much about you at all."

"We've known each other for years."

"And yet, I don't know much about you."

"Hmm." He focused on the DJ as he sipped his drink. I focused on his guarded expression.

"Not very forthcoming," I said after a moment.

"What would you like to know?" He glanced at me. "Just ask."

"I guess I don't have a specific question." I took another sip of my drink. "Do you really travel with Kayla everywhere?"

"No, and if she approaches you again, you should probably have

Amir or whoever you're with intervene."

"She seemed pretty harmless."

"I'm not saying she'd harm you physically, but there's no use subjecting yourself to things like that. From anyone."

"Things like what? She seemed like a hurt girlfriend or something." I bit my lip, hoping I was wrong about that.

The only examples of good men I had were the ones in my life, and none of them were saints. My father had more affairs than I probably knew about. My brother Aramis admittedly grew bored with women quickly and was always chasing after a new one. Thankfully, my eldest brother, Elias, had met someone he couldn't live without, and I knew without a doubt that he'd remain faithful to her. Still, men like Benjamin Drake were the untamable type. The ones you definitely fooled around with but never settled down with—not for lack of trying. Even though I was okay with those things, I was definitely not all right with being the other woman.

"She's not my girlfriend," Ben said after a long, quiet moment. "Never was, never will be. But I have traveled with her in the past."

"Not this time though?"

"She attended my gala the other night, even though I asked you to join me. I'm sure she stayed longer to soak up the party scene before heading home."

"Where's home?"

"Paris."

"Hmm." I licked my lips. "She didn't seem Parisian."

"She's Israeli."

"Like you."

"Like me." He smiled.

"I have a personal question."

"Sure." He drained what was left in his glass and looked at mine. "Want a refill while you interrogate me?"

"Sure." I handed him my empty glass and wondered if this felt like an interrogation. That term always held a negative connotation. "Are you sleeping with her?"

"I'm not. I haven't in a long time. That ship has sailed. I did invite her to the gala, but as a friend."

"She has a picture of you together as the lock screen on her phone. I'm pretty sure she disagrees."

"Well, that's Kayla for you." He chuckled, shaking his head as he handed me my drink and took his own. "We met when we were young. She kind of clung to me, and I let her because I liked feeling needed. But what we had was closer to a long-term one-night stand than an actual relationship."

"Isn't that what relationships technically are? Long one-night stands?"

"Not if you don't partake in pillow talk."

"And you don't."

"Not really." He looked at the DJ, who was announcing another DJ soon to take his place on stage.

"You asked me a lot of questions," I said.

"I don't consider you a one-night stand."

"What about Sophia," I asked, mentioning the actress he used to date. "You were with her for a while."

"Sophia and I were barely ever in the same city. That was another long one-night stand without much pillow talk. She's a great woman, but not right for me."

"So, who is?" I leaned in a little closer so I didn't have to shout.

He looked over at me and smiled. We were sitting very close now, our knees brushing, our noses nearly touching. He studied my eyes for a long time, so long I was sure he'd forgotten I'd asked him a question. I held my breath. Waited. Bit my lip. His gaze dropped to my mouth, my body heating as he met my eyes again. He set his drink down on the table in front of us without breaking eye contact and brought one hand to my face, then the other, coming closer. I thought my heart might seize in my chest as he inched closer still, his eyes searching mine, his breath tickling my nose.

"I think you're right for me," he said, his voice low just before he pressed his lips to mine.

Our tongues met, and the kiss deepened. The taste of his alcohol mixed with mine made me feel as if I could die right there from happiness.

Chapter Thirteen

Ben

I couldn't seem to get enough of her. I'd anticipated that being the case, but I couldn't have predicted the way being with her would make me feel. It was one thing to admire her from mostly afar all of the time and feel flattered that she showed interest in me. Having her all to myself was something else altogether. It reminded me of what I felt every time I stepped a foot on the pitch, ready to chase the ball. It was thrilling and unknown, and I wanted to explore as much of it as she'd let me. Not even her questions annoyed me, which was normally the case with every woman I dated. They always wanted to know too much and would question my relationship with Kayla once they found out about her, which was common. Kayla liked to introduce herself to every woman I was seen with. Like I'd assured Pilar, she was harmless. David thought I was an idiot for letting her come around and for inviting her to the gala this weekend. She'd been the one to give me the idea for the foundation though. I couldn't use the suggestion and then not invite her to the celebration for it. As if listening to my thoughts, David appeared in my line of sight. I pulled away from Pilar and smiled at the desire painted on her face.

"My friends are here," I said.

"Oh." She straightened and fixed her hair.

David's eyebrows rose. I couldn't wipe the smile off my face as I stood to greet him. We clasped hands and bumped shoulders.

"This looks like the exact opposite of what I told you to do," he said as he patted my back and pulled away to greet Pilar.

"We've met," she said, smiling as she stood. "David, right?"

"That's right. We met at one of your mother's Sunday dinners." He smiled at her, then looked at me. Warren and Camila are parking."

"Nice." I looked over at Pilar, whose eyes had widened. I chuckled, remembering that she was actually an avid football fan. "Yes, Warren Silva."

"Oh my God." She smiled the biggest smile I'd ever seen. It was cute, especially since Warren was a happily married family man with two small children.

"I'll get a photo of you with him." I winked.

"That would be epic." She took a sip of her drink, seemingly unable to wipe the smile off her face.

"You know who else is coming?" David said, playfully taunting Pilar now. "Alex Scott."

"No." Her mouth dropped. She faced me with a wicked smile that turned me inside out. "You may just have some competition tonight."

"Is that so?" I raised an eyebrow.

I knew she was joking, but I didn't like where this was going. If anyone else had made that comment, I would have dismissed both the comment and the woman right away. But Pilar saying it made me see red. Alex was one of my best friends and would never come between a woman and me, but he also loved to fuck with me. If he knew how much I liked Pilar, he'd purposely flirt with her to get a rise out of me. I mentally prepared myself for that.

"We'll have to see how I feel when he gets here." Pilar winked.

David laughed, thoroughly enjoying this. I scowled. A few things happened all at once. David said he was going to say hi to some people and would be back. The DJ played a rendition of Bazzi's *Paradise,* and Pilar started dancing. I watched her for a moment, loving the way she moved her hips, her hands waving in the air, and her eyes closed as she sang along. She was simply beautiful when she was like this, and I felt privileged to see this side of her. Before I could stop myself, I pulled her to me and began dancing with her, my hands on her hips, my mouth near her ear. I couldn't remember the last time a woman had made me feel this way, where sharing the same space was excitement enough, and the fact that I'd be taking her home tonight was the cherry on top. When Warren walked in holding Camila's hand, I looked over and nodded at him in greeting. He did the same, and Camila waved and smiled. She was already moving her hips to the music, and I knew they'd join us dancing in the small area of the VIP section soon enough. When the song was over, I introduced them to Pilar.

"Am I supposed to bow or something?" Camila asked, tentatively holding out her hand for Pilar to shake.

Pilar laughed and stepped forward to give Camila a kiss on both cheeks.

"That's easy," Camila said, smiling. "Nice to meet you. I've never met royalty before."

"She's not royalty this weekend." I winked at Pilar. She blushed, smiling widely. "She's just a regular citizen like the rest of us."

"Cool." Warren smiled. "I like what your brother is doing in Paris. Not that I live there, but I keep up with the news."

"Where do you live now?" Pilar asked.

"Ah, a little place called Harlem. It's in New York." Warren grinned. "Little gem of a place."

"It *is* a gem of a place, actually." Camila elbowed him hard, but all it did was make him laugh harder. She smiled at Pilar. "You guys should come visit someday."

"Uh, yeah. Maybe." Pilar smiled, but I could tell she was thrown by the invitation, mostly because when Camila invited you somewhere, it was obvious that she meant it.

"We'll definitely go one day." I grabbed Pilar's hand in mine and squeezed it. She met my gaze with a look of surprise.

Warren, Camila, Pilar, and I sat down and started talking, leaning over each other to hear over the loud music. David joined us shortly after, and then, Alex arrived, completely charming Pilar and Camila. Both of them were blushing and sharing looks until Warren and I were about ready to kick Alex out of the group.

"Who invited this guy?" Warren asked loudly after a moment.

"Your mother," Alex said.

I laughed.

The women laughed louder.

"I think it's great that he's here," Pilar said.

"Of course, you do." I scowled.

Alex's brows rose, and I instantly knew my mistake. He threw an arm over Pilar's shoulder.

"So, how are you enjoying Ibiza? Is it your first time?"

"I love it." She turned ten shades of red.

I grabbed my supposed best friend's arm and pushed it off my date, shooting him a look.

"*What?*" he mouthed, pretending to be innocent.

"I will cut you." I shot him a look.

He laughed loudly, shaking his head. "This is great."

We talked, danced, drank, danced some more, drank some more.

"Where are the kids?" I asked Warren. "Back home?"

"Yeah. We left them with our mothers, which is a nightmare in itself." He shook his head.

"My mom called me a little while ago and said the baby may or may not have a diaper rash, and that she was going to make him a tea to put on the affected area," Camila said, sighing. "I can't even."

"Tea on the baby's bottom?" Pilar frowned. "Why?"

"Because she wouldn't put Vicks there, and since that's the number one cure for everything in a Dominican household and she can't do it, tea with all these weird herbs is a close second."

"Oh my God." Pilar laughed. "That's great. It's nice that she worries."

"Too much." Camila shook her head. "My sister is going through a nasty divorce, and she has a three-year-old, so I don't want to bother her. But I'm dying for her to take the kids to her house."

"That sucks. I didn't know Vanessa was getting a divorce," I said. I'd met her and her husband a handful of times, and they were always nice.

"Yeah. That's life, I guess." Camila shrugged.

"Not our life." Warren grabbed her hand and leaned in to kiss her. "Don't get any ideas."

"Trust me, I would have left you by now." She laughed at his expression.

Alex and I watched wistfully. Warren had been our hero for so long on the pitch, but off the field, he scored serious goals, with a beautiful woman on his arm and two adorable children. He ran a successful foundation and did business in New York as well as in Spain. He was what all of us were trying to be, even though it felt unattainable. I glanced at Pilar, who was now drinking water, and wondered how she'd feel if I told her that was my goal. Would she run for the hills? She was young and innocent, maybe she wouldn't want any of that right now. Not to mention, she was a princess. That complicated things. I wasn't even sure why I was wondering about this or cared how she'd feel. It wasn't like she could be a long-term goal, regardless of how she made me feel.

Chapter Fourteen

Ben

"I had so much fun." She sighed beside me as I drove to my place.

"Good." I set my hand over hers.

"I think I'm drunk."

"I think you are too." I chuckled.

"Are we going back to your place?"

"Yep."

"Are you going to take advantage of me?" She brought my hand up to her lips and sucked my pointer into her mouth.

"No." I groaned.

"I want you to." She sucked it again.

"Pilar." I let out a shaky breath as I parked the car in the garage and closed the big door behind us. "As tempting as you are, I'd rather wait to take advantage of you when you're not drunk."

"But I want you to," she repeated.

"And I will…when you're sober." I took back my hand and cupped her face with it, leaning in to kiss her deeply.

She tasted of vodka and orange. Like the sweetest sin I'd ever been tempted with. When I pulled away, she mumbled an argument, but I led her out of the car and into my villa nonetheless. I'd have her again, but tonight wasn't the time for that. I wouldn't discount the morning though.

Inside, I gave her something for the headache she'd likely have tomorrow. I helped her in the bathroom as she undressed for a shower. I'd never shown more restraint in my life, of that I was sure. Once we were both clean and dressed in one of his t-shirts, we lay in bed. I pulled her to me and enjoyed the sound of her soft breath. I was sure I'd never felt this level of peace before.

"Tell me something no one else knows about you," she whispered.

"Are we having a heart-to-heart?" I whispered back.

She glanced up at me. "Is that okay?"

I'd never been the most forthcoming man, mostly because I'd seen what happened to people who let their guards down. Vulnerability was a virus. The moment you let your control slip, you became exposed to attack in ways you never imagined.

"Something no one else knows," I said, letting myself savor the idea of opening up fully to this woman who had bared herself to me. "I had a brother." I swallowed. "He died when I first came into the league. The year we won the championship. Everyone was elated, celebrating, while I was mourning. Maybe that's why winning always tastes bitter to me."

"I'm so sorry." She glanced up and met my eyes. "I can't imagine losing a sibling."

"It's pretty unimaginable." I exhaled, holding her closer.

"How'd he...how did he die?"

"He was killed while documenting a war zone."

"I'm so sorry." She sat up straighter, no longer lounging against me. I instantly missed her warmth.

"As I mentioned at the gala, he was a photojournalist, and that was his passion. We all knew the risks, but it was still hard. The specific area he was in was supposed to be safe. He saw a lot those days, lived more lives than most of us, experienced loss the way I hope neither of us ever have to." I swallowed, letting myself tell this story aloud for the first time. "They said it was suicide, not a war act, but I don't believe that."

"Maybe...maybe he witnessed too much pain?"

"Perhaps. Or maybe someone killed him because he saw too much. Either way, he's gone, and we never even got his body back to give him a proper burial. It doesn't matter. I just hate to think that my brother, my best friend, wouldn't turn to me in a time of need."

"I get that." She set her hand over mine. "I'm sorry. Thank you for sharing that with me."

I smiled softly.

"Did he ever see you play?"

"He came to a lot of my games." I smiled. "He was my biggest supporter."

"I'm sure you miss him."

"More than anything."

She held me tighter. "I wish I could've met him."

"He would have loved you."

"Yeah?"

"Definitely."

"Would you have introduced us? It seems like you don't introduce many women to your family." She looked at me again. "Am I right about that?"

"You are."

"Yet you would have introduced us?"

"Definitely." I kissed the top of her head.

I wasn't just saying that because she was lying in my arms. I was serious. Pilar was the kind of woman I'd want to introduce to everyone in my life. She was kind and good and beautiful and made me feel things I hadn't allowed myself to feel in a long time, if ever. I wasn't sure what to make of that or where to go from here, but I knew I wanted to keep her in my arms like this for as long as possible.

Chapter Fifteen

Pilar

"Someone is here to see you." Amir's voice made my eyes snap open.

I yawned. I must have dozed off at some point in the middle of writing my letter. Elias and Adeline asked me to write missives to children for the first day of school, which was coming up. "*Write something inspiring that'll make them want to learn,*" they'd said. I'd always been a superb student, but I never needed outside inspiration to make that happen. I just did what I knew I was supposed to do, and getting good grades was one of those things. And now, at this point in my life, I still wasn't sure how I felt about children in general, so this was an interesting exercise. I set the paper and pen aside and walked out of my room, eyeing Amir suspiciously.

"Who's here to see me?"

"I am. I hope you don't mind."

My heart beat a little faster at the sound of Ben's voice, and when I walked all the way into the foyer and saw him, I thought it would go into a frenzy. He was dressed casually in jeans and a white button-down, the sleeves rolled to the elbows. I'd never really thought much about arms. I'd always been a back girl, but Ben's forearms were quite possibly the sexiest thing I'd ever seen on a man. And that was saying something, given the rest of him.

"I don't mind at all." I smiled, remembering myself, then looked at the bag he carried. "Did you bring food?"

"Wine, cheese, and ham."

"That sounds wonderful." I looked at the dining room, but it seemed too boring and formal. The kitchen could work, but the chefs were nosey and congregated there, and I'd rather not have an audience. Finally, I turned to my bedroom. It had ample space and a sitting area as well as a balcony—and memories of what we'd done there. I felt myself blush and pushed the thought away quickly. "Amir, will you have someone bring us plates, a bottle opener, and—"

"Glasses," he said. "I'm on it."

A few minutes later, Amir walked in with those things and set them on the table before signaling to me that he'd be around. I thanked him and waved as he closed the door behind him. Ben stood by the window, looking out at the ocean beneath us.

"Do you want to open the doors?" I moved to do just that, but he took over and pushed them wide. He then moved the table a little closer to the balcony. I grinned. "Perfect."

"I think so." He smiled at me, and I got the feeling he wasn't talking about the outside view.

We sat down, side by side. He opened the bottle of wine while I uncovered what he'd brought with him—cheeses, ham, jam, bread. Everything looked so good, my stomach began to rumble.

"I guess I was hungry, after all." My cheeks warmed as I ate a slice of cheese.

"I'm always hungry." He winked at me as he poured the wine.

"Thanks."

"Cheers." He raised his glass to mine. "To the unexpected."

I clinked my glass to his and took a sip before setting it down. "What's unexpected?"

"You."

"And what about me is unexpected?" I raised an eyebrow.

"Absolutely everything, Princess." He placed a hand over mine. "Unexpected, yet welcome."

"Not so unexpected if you specifically asked for me to be your date at the gala."

"Well, I'd like to think we were sort of friends before this summer." He met my eyes. "But I'm not sure that friends share this much chemistry or have such an attraction to each other."

"If they did, I imagine they'd become more than friends."

"If they're lucky."

"Are you?"

"Lucky?" he asked. I nodded. He chuckled. "Right now, I feel like the luckiest man alive."

"I feel pretty lucky, as well."

He grinned at me and looked out at the ocean. "Do you like the freedom that being here brings?"

"I do." I looked over at him. "Not as much as you do, I'm sure."

"I'm not used to being in the spotlight."

"I can't say what it would be like to be away from it for too long. Even when the cameras aren't flashing and the paparazzi aren't chasing, we're always putting on an act for someone."

"Even during Sunday dinners?"

"Especially during Sunday dinners." I laughed, shrugging. "I guess it depends on who's there."

"When I'm there, you're always the perfect little host. Quiet and attentive. Who would have known that underneath it all, you're such a naughty princess?"

I bit my lip as he came closer, brushing his nose against mine. "I'm only naughty when you're around."

"Is that so?"

"Yes."

"I probably shouldn't like hearing that as much as I do," he murmured against me, nipping my lower lip and pulling it into his mouth. My body was on fire. I set my glass down and moved closer, wrapping my arms around him, wishing I could wrap myself around him completely. He moved his chair and welcomed me onto his lap, his fingers deftly pushing up the summer dress I wore. He found my center quickly.

"We should go inside," I whisper-panted against his mouth, though my hips rocked, clearly not agreeing.

"Should we?"

"Yes." I gasped as his fingers entered me.

"Should I stop?"

"God, no." My head dropped back.

I didn't want him to stop. Ever.

* * * *

Ben and I had been inseparable. So much so, that Joslyn had been in town for two days and I hadn't even seen her. So, when I walked into my room and saw her, I shrieked.

"Did you forget I was here?" She raised an eyebrow as she looked up at me.

"Honestly? Yes." I took a deep breath as I lowered my hand from my pounding heart.

"Well, I haven't wanted to bother you. I figured if you needed me, you'd call." She smiled. "You look…happy."

She was sitting in the comfortable leather recliner in the corner of my bedroom, and had been reading a newspaper like an old man. It was people like Joss who kept the newspaper industry going, so I never made fun of her for it, but she really did look funny with her reading glasses and paper.

"I am happy." I sighed, opening my arms and letting myself fall smack into the middle of the plush, king-size bed.

"Do tell." The paper crinkled, and the footrest of the leather chair clicked back into place.

"I don't even know where to start." I turned on my side so I could look at her.

"Well, you haven't been back to the villa in two days now. Start there."

"It's been like a never-ending date." I smiled widely.

"Are you going to share?"

"Well, I mean, you want details? I can't give you all the details."

"With the way you're blushing, I want them, but I won't ask because I don't want you to hide from me for the next few days. I was getting bored here all alone."

"I really like him."

"Pilar." There was a warning note in her tone.

"I know. I know."

"We said fun. You'd have fun while you're here. Sometimes, you don't get to take the fun home."

"I know." I shut my eyes to that reality.

She wasn't wrong. As wanted as Ben had made me feel, I knew this was temporary. It had to be. Now that I'd taken on more responsibilities with the Crown, anyone I dated would be put in the limelight, and from what I knew about Ben, that was the last thing he wanted.

"Imagine how it'll be at your mother's Sunday dinners if you don't fully accept that it's temporary," she said.

"Yeah, you're right." I opened my eyes again. "But I also want to remind you that you were wrong about Elias and Adeline."

"I was, wasn't I?" She frowned slightly. "But that was because your brother stepped up and did something about it. He was in a position where he could. Ben...well, he'd have to want to settle down. Do you think he wants to settle down?"

"I'm not sure. He doesn't seem opposed to it." I gave her a small smile. "But I also don't want to spring that on him. He likes to keep his private life private." I shrugged.

"And that's an impossible task with the Crown," she said.

I nodded sadly.

"Well, let's wait for him to decide what he wants." She sighed. "Sometimes, love chooses for you."

"Love?" I felt my eyes widen. "I don't think he's... I don't think we're..." I paused. "It's too soon for love."

"Love has no time restraints." She shot me a look. "But I'm not going to encourage this. I'm not supposed to, and I won't. I'm supposed to talk sense into you and tell you that it's dumb, not tell you to be open to it."

"Spoken like a true secretary of the Crown," I said, though I meant it sarcastically.

I'd never second-guessed anything, but lately, I'd been doing that with every situation. I was beginning to dislike the idea that we had been brought to this Earth for one sole purpose, and that was to serve the Crown. I wanted to serve myself for once. I couldn't even imagine how it was for Elias, who had the weight of so much responsibility on his shoulders—from the time he was born. The only thing I wanted was Ben, and every moment I spent with him, I only wanted him more and more. But the fact of who I was made it all seem pretty impossible.

Chapter Sixteen

Pilar

"Did you tell Ben to drive you?"

"What?" I glanced up at Amir, who was standing in the threshold of my room. "No. I told him I had to go home this weekend to do a few things and that I'd be back on Monday."

"Well, his security called us and said he's on his way here because he's taking you to the airport."

"I mean, I'm not opposed." I smiled. More time with Ben was definitely something I wouldn't turn down.

"He'll be here in ten minutes. Are you ready?"

"Ready."

I was due back in Paris for a quick trip. Joss had left earlier this morning to take care of some things with Aramis. Apparently, he'd locked an heiress he'd been on a date with out of his apartment and then left her out there pounding on the door while paparazzi photographed her. I swear, my brother Elias was close to putting Aramis on *The Bachelor: Eligible Prince Edition* if he didn't start coming to his senses. I hadn't even asked Adeline if she'd spoken to my brother about my situation with Ben. I didn't want anyone to burst my bubble and tell me that he was too much for me—older, more experienced, etcetera. Being with him made me feel safe and free, and the thought of giving any of that up made me want to cry. I heard the rev of a car's engine as Ben pulled up to the front of the house and felt myself smile.

"Hey," I said upon exiting the villa and seeing the black sports car.

"I hope you don't mind that I hijacked Amir's job." Ben got out of the driver's seat and walked over to the passenger door, opening it as he waited for me to approach. When I reached him, he wrapped an arm around me and pulled me flush against him, kissing me deeply before letting me go.

"How could I mind?" I ducked into the car and waited for him to close the door. I looked out at Amir, who was shaking his head with a chuckle. "I'll see you there."

He jogged over to the SUV behind us and took the wheel, following us as Ben drove off. He placed a hand over mine, which was currently resting on my knee.

"I don't know what I'm going to do without you while you're gone."

"I'll only be gone a couple of days." I grinned so widely, it made my face hurt. "I'm sure you'll find someone else to occupy your time."

"Definitely not." He squeezed my hand, looking into my eyes as he stopped at a red light. "I'm waiting for you."

"That probably shouldn't make me as happy as it does, but here we are." I winked at him. "When are you due back in Paris for training?"

"One week." He sighed. "I love football. It's my favorite thing in the world, but the older I get, the more my joints hurt when I think about going out there for an entire season."

I laughed. "You're getting old, Drake."

"I guess I am." He pinched me playfully. "Not too old for you, I hope."

"I guess I have a thing for older men." I bit my lip as I looked over at him. "Or maybe just older men named Benjamin Drake."

"Good answer." He brought my hand up and kissed it as he pulled into the parking lot where the private jet hangars were located.

After Amir had settled everything with our identification, we drove in and parked in front of the small office. Ben got out and opened the door for me, holding my hand as he walked me inside.

"We're ready," Amir announced, walking away from the counter and toward us.

"I guess this is goodbye." I faced Ben.

"Not goodbye. I'll see you soon." He kissed me then, and I wrapped my arms around him to deepen the kiss because I felt like I needed to savor this moment to make up for all of the ones I'd miss over the weekend.

It was a dangerous feeling, but I couldn't help it. I couldn't stop myself from falling, and at this point, I wasn't sure I wanted to try.

* * * *

I'd only been in Paris a few short hours before I reported for my first duty. I was serving food at one of the local homeless shelters today. It had always been one of my favorite places to come as a kid. My parents would bring my brothers and I every Christmas. Even though we were extremely privileged, and Santa never skipped our houses, serving food for the less fortunate put things into perspective. The shelter was also one of the few places that always supported my father, regardless of what the rest of the country said about him. When my brother stepped into the role of king, they were very vocal in their praise. And when he chose to marry Adeline, a commoner, they were even more so. Amir and I pulled up to the shelter, and he switched off the car.

"Are you sure you want to drive home by yourself?"

"Please. It's only two blocks, and I need my space." I smiled. "Besides, Aramis is coming to serve food with me, so I'll be safe." I winked.

Amir nodded as we stepped out of the car, and he jogged over to the waiting SUV with the other security members. The thing I loved about Paris was that, yes, we were always flanked by security, but in instances like these, where we were close to home and at a safe place, we were allowed some freedom. It wasn't much, but when you lived under a microscope, you learned to appreciate every bit of it. As I walked to the door, I sent my brother a text, telling him I would wait for him inside. On the rare occasion where we felt extra daring, we stood outside for a while with no security, hiding behind sunglasses and beneath hats. Today, I just wanted to go inside and do my duty so that I could go home and sleep in my bed. My phone vibrated, and I stopped walking, unlocking the screen to find a text, though not from my brother.

Ben: I hope you had a good flight. I miss you already.

I took a deep breath and smiled, reveling in those words. Ben missed me, and it wasn't like he had to tell me as much. He could have played it cool like most guys I knew. Instead, he'd sent me a message, telling me that he missed me. I bit my lip as I responded.

Me: I miss you too. I wish I had thought to kidnap you and bring you in my suitcase.

Ben: I saw the size of your suitcase. I think I'd fit.

Me: haha. I think you might!

Ben: I wouldn't have been opposed to going home to be with you.

Butterflies took flight in my belly. I bit my lip harder.

"I'm surprised he let you out of his sight."

I gasped at the sound of Kayla's voice and glanced up to find her standing a few feet away from me. "What are you doing here?"

"I live in the area." She shrugged. "I heard you were going to come feed the poor today. It must be tedious work, considering you don't even feed yourself."

My pulse quickened. "What do you want?"

"What do I want? Nothing. I'm just taking a walk."

"You should leave."

"I will." She looked past me. "Nice car. Are you sure you want to leave it parked in a neighborhood like this?"

The shelter doors opened before I could form a response, and Monsieur Baron stepped outside.

"Pilar! We've been expecting you." He smiled.

"*Bonjour.*" I smiled back, then looked at Kayla. "I have to go. I have important people to meet with."

She glowered at me but walked away. I strolled inside, trying to brush off the encounter. The papers always published where we'd be making appearances for the Crown, so I wasn't shocked that she knew where I'd be. But the fact that she'd followed me here was unsettling. I made a note to tell Amir about it. Our previous encounter had been uncomfortable, but this was more than that. Soon enough, Monsieur Baron set me up behind the counter, and Aramis walked in, flashing me a big smile.

"I've been waiting for you." I shot him a look.

"I was busy kicking someone out of bed." He winked.

"You were? Or Joss was?" I raised an eyebrow.

"Joslyn has become a major pain in my butt." He pulled on a white apron, walked over to me, and squeezed me into a hug. "I've missed you. How was your holiday?"

"It's not over. I'm going back in two days. But it's splendid so far. Everything I ever dreamed of. I don't know why I didn't start going sooner."

"Because you're too much of a good girl to rebel." He pulled away.

"So, anything you want to tell me?"

"No." I blushed despite myself and looked away quickly. Had Ben told my brother about us? They were friends, after all. "Do you have something you want to tell *me*?"

"Aside from the fact that I'm dying to drive that shiny new car of yours? Nope."

"You can drive it to my place. I'll drive yours." I bumped his hip with mine as we started serving food on the plates. "How have Elias and Adeline been?"

"Oh, you know, trying to control the kingdom, but fine."

"They are not controlling, Aramis." I laughed. "You just don't want to change, and that's a problem for the family right now."

"So, I'm a problem?"

"Honestly? Yes."

"How?" he scoffed.

"Eli asked us not to call attention to ourselves, and that's all you've been doing."

"Really? Because unlike all of you, I happen to read the papers, and they're all talking about how you're partying too hard in Ibiza."

"Ibiza is a party." I rolled my eyes. "It's not my fault they have nothing else to talk about right now."

"That's exactly how I feel about my situation."

I smiled at the woman taking the plate in front of me and small-talked momentarily with her before turning back to my brother. "Your situation is entirely different. For starters, the women you sleep with are famous in their own right, and you treat them like crap. Publicly."

"Yet they keep coming back." He shrugged a shoulder.

"What you need is a swift kick in the butt. A woman who comes out of nowhere and makes you settle down once and for all."

"Good luck with that. All the good ones are taken," he scoffed.

"Joss isn't taken."

He opened his mouth and then closed it, frowning before shaking his head. "Joslyn hates me."

"I never understood why."

"We all have our secrets." He shot me a look that spoke volumes, and I shut my mouth about love for the remainder of our time at the shelter. The last thing I needed was my brother lecturing me about Ben, and I was pretty sure he knew all about us.

Chapter Seventeen

Pilar

I couldn't stop laughing at the show my brother was putting on as he got inside my sparkly red sports car. He was acting like his car wasn't just as luxurious. I shook my head from behind the wheel of his SUV and placed my phone on the magnetic holder he had tucked into the air vent. We all had them, a gift from Joslyn last year, so that when we were driving, we could still talk on the phone. I dialed my brother and saw him do the same thing with his phone in my car as he answered.

"Your seat is up to the steering wheel."

"That's because I'm much shorter than you." I snapped on my seatbelt and fixed his seat so that it was closer to the steering wheel. "This is a safe car. A total dad car, if you ask me."

"Dad car?" He chuckled. "I guess my Range Rover would be lame in comparison to this R8."

"I agree."

"We're going to your place, right?"

"Yep. Unless you want to go get dinner. Or go to Eli and Addie's."

"Didn't you just get in? Have you even been home?"

"Not yet." I watched as the brake lights of my car flickered on, which meant he was about to start driving. I put the SUV into drive, as well.

"Are you hungry? We can get food delivered and tell Eli and Addie to meet us there."

"That sounds like a better idea," I agreed. "I'm going to call the little Chinese place by my house and order."

"Okay. I'll call Eli."

We hung up and started to drive. Aramis peeled out of the parking spot with a loud rev of the engine, and I tried to follow with as much gusto, but his Range Rover wasn't up to that kind of speed—too heavy. We reached the first light and passed it, then made a right. As we approached the second light, which crossed between a major street and the exit of the highway, I saw that we had five seconds to beat the yellow light that was approaching, and knew Aramis would slam the accelerator. I prepared to do the same, adrenaline coursing through me as we neared. I heard the engine of the car in front of me, felt the one of the vehicle I was in, but knew we wouldn't beat the yellow. It would turn red as we passed, if we were lucky. It all played out in slow motion, the way one watches a movie that's both terrifying and intriguing, a train wreck you can't quite look away from.

Aramis floored it. The vehicle, which was the safest in its class, swerved left and right before spinning out of control in the middle of the red. I slammed on my brakes, gasping as my heart hit my throat, watching in anticipation, hoping like hell he'd regain control before the intersection opened up to the street.

I felt as if the world stopped as one vehicle, then another crashed into the car Aramis was driving. The car I was supposed to be driving. I didn't think about my surroundings as I got out of the car and ran over to him. I didn't think about how crowded the streets were or that I myself could also be hurt doing this.

The only thing I could think about was my brother.

Chapter Eighteen

Ben

"Have you seen the news?" David asked, walking into the villa.

"No. What happened?" I switched the channel.

"Prince Aramis and Princess Pilar involved in fatal car accident"

Fatal car accident.

The control slipped out of my hand, crashing to the floor.

"In critical condition."

"Ben?"

I blinked, looking at David, my eyes glazed and hazy.

"Do you want to go?" David asked.

I thought I nodded. I thought I said something. I couldn't be sure. I felt numb. I'd just seen her. I'd just texted with her a couple of hours ago. I glanced up at the television, took in the helicopter footage as it circulated around the scene. My heart squeezed. God, please no. I'd give her up if it meant she'd be okay. I'd give up football. I'd give up anything to rewind time so that she could be okay. That was the mantra I kept in my head the entire flight over and on my way to the hospital when we finally got there. Nothing else mattered, I realized. And as I stepped out of the SUV and into the sea of swarming cameras taking my picture, I no longer cared. I didn't care to hide behind a wall. I cared about Pilar, getting to Pilar and making sure she was okay. It was the only thing I cared about in that moment.

* * * *

"What are you doing here?" Elias turned to me when he saw me in the hall. Two of his security personnel stepped between us.

"Are they okay? Is Aramis okay? Pilar? What happened?"

"They're…they're going to be fine." Elias's expression fell. He waved away the security team between us and let me come closer. "Aramis was driving Pilar's car and it spun out of control." He shook his head. "She went to try and help, and was hit by a cyclist and fell, but she's okay. He's fine. He just got out of surgery, and he's all right."

"What about the fire? It looked like there was a fire."

"One of the cars…" Elias swallowed. "One of the other cars involved caught fire."

"And the fatalities?" I held my breath, feeling like every single thing out of his mouth was the most important thing I'd ever heard.

"Two people died." He looked down.

"Hey." Adeline walked out of one of the rooms and headed toward us. "Ben, are you here to see…?"

"Pi—I'm here for both of them," I said, because it was the truth. I would have been here for Aramis, but I ran here, flew here, for Pilar.

"She's in there," Adeline whispered, pointing at the room she'd just left.

She put her hand in Elias's and pulled him to the chairs in the waiting area. That was when I noticed that Elias's mother was also there, sitting and speaking to some people. Our eyes met, and I gave her what I hoped was a sympathetic look. She acknowledged it with a nod and then returned her attention to those she had been talking to.

I opened the door slowly and stopped breathing when I saw Pilar on the hospital bed, Amir at her side. He looked as if he'd lost hours of sleep and gained hundreds of years since the last time I saw him. He glanced up at me and walked toward the door, setting a hand on my shoulder as he left. I walked forward quickly and went over to Pilar.

"Hey." She smiled weakly. "I'm fine. I just…scratches." She pointed at the scratch on her face and lifted her arms to show light bruising. "But my brother…" Her eyes welled with tears. "Aramis."

"He's fine. He's stable. Just got out of surgery," I said, grabbing her hands in mine and taking a seat beside her in the small bed. I looked at her and felt myself crumble as I leaned in and wrapped my arms around her as gently as I could. "You scared the hell out of me, Princess." I pulled away. "Are you really okay? What happened?"

"I'm fine. I feel fine. I'll be out of here tomorrow. I just…" Her lip wobbled. "Aramis."

"He really is okay." I squeezed her hand. "I'm going to go see him next, but your brother is fine. You know he's too stubborn to leave us."

"I know." She laughed and hiccupped as a tear fell down her face. "It was so scary."

I nodded. It *was* scary, and I hadn't even been involved. The lump in my throat hadn't left, not even now that I was here with her and knew she was all right. It was a reminder of how short and fragile life was, that I could lose her the way I'd lost my brother. I couldn't handle it. Not her. I squeezed her hand tighter.

"What are you doing here?" she whispered, wiping a tear.

"I came to see you. I left as soon as I saw the news. I couldn't just…" I exhaled. "I couldn't stand the thought of losing you, not like this."

She smiled weakly and squeezed my hand back, then lost her smile altogether. "Kayla was there."

"Where?"

"At the shelter. Aramis and I went to feed the homeless today, and she was outside." Pilar frowned. "She said something about me not leaving my car there. Do you think…?" She looked up at me.

"No." I felt myself frown. *What could Kayla have possibly done to the car?* In the grand scheme of things, it didn't matter what she could have done or not, I needed to put an end to the stalking. "She wouldn't. She couldn't. How was the car before the accident?"

"It was perfect. It only had three hundred miles on it. It was brand new."

"I'll put an end to this Kayla stuff," I said.

"I told Amir about it just in case. I just…it seems crazy and far-fetched, I know, but I can't stop thinking about it."

"She won't come near you again." I kissed her hand, feeling like I never wanted to let go.

The weight of that pushed at me, sat heavily on my chest. I needed to tell her things if I was going to keep her in my life. I needed to be vocal and open up. This wasn't the time for it, though. I needed her to focus on getting better first.

Chapter Nineteen

Pilar

"I heard you're dating Drake." Aramis's voice was dry and low.

His words made me laugh, and then cry, and then laugh again. My brother looked awful, and I wasn't just saying that because he was lying on a hospital bed with a cast on his left leg, and his left shoulder covered in bindings. His face was filled with tiny scratches from the broken windshield, and bandages covered the burns he'd acquired from the car that'd caught fire. Yet he was alive, and he was here, and he'd heal and be fine again, at least according to the doctors and surgeons. We were lucky. Two people had died, yet Aramis had somehow made it out of it.

"I'm so sorry." I squeezed his hand. "If I'd been driving…"

"Don't." He shot me a look. "Don't even think it. I would never trade places with you. I wouldn't allow it. You're my baby sister, and I need you to be safe. Always. I'm fine."

"You're not." I began to sob, my chest heaving. "You're completely messed up."

"I'm always messed up, darling." He winked, then flinched.

"Stop it." I laughed as tears ran down my cheeks. I sniffled and wiped at them. "I told Amir to look into what happened. Ben has a crazy ex, and she confronted me before I went into the shelter. She knew which vehicle was mine. Knew that I was there alone."

"You think she did something?"

"I don't know what to think." I exhaled. "I don't know. What could she have done? Tampered with the engine? The brakes?"

"No." He shook his head and then winced a bit. "It was none of those. It was almost as if...it was like the car couldn't stay straight."

"The tires?" I asked. I'd driven Audis for most of my adult life and I'd gotten flat tires on them. They weren't quick to give out, even with a nail embedded in them. I said that aloud, and Aramis shook his head.

"This wasn't a nail, Pilar. It had to be a slash."

My heart stopped beating. "Could she want me out of Ben's life that badly?"

"She must." He stared at me for a beat. "The question is, do you want to be in this relationship badly enough to put up with people like her?"

My knee-jerk response was "*of course*," but seeing my brother like this...I wasn't so sure.

"How'd that happen anyway?" he asked.

"What?"

"You and Ben."

"That's really the first thing you're going to ask me about?" I laughed. "We'll talk about it later."

"I think it's worth discussing now, seeing as I have nowhere to go." His lip twitched, but his eyes were dull and remained sad.

"Well." I cleared my throat. "It just happened. I guess it started as us just having fun, but it may have become something more."

"You guess?" Aramis raised his eyebrows and cringed with pain. "Are you having fun or not? It's that simple."

"I am."

"But it's not serious? Or is it?"

"We haven't discussed it." I worried my bottom lip. "It's Ben, you know. He has a reputation, and it certainly isn't about being a serious boyfriend."

"Just because he hasn't been in a serious relationship, doesn't mean he doesn't want one." He tilted his head. "Besides, he flew here the minute he heard that you were in the hospital."

"He came to see you too."

"I'm pretty sure he came here for you." He winked. "He didn't sleep beside my bed all night."

"That's true." I worried my lip.

It was true, wasn't it? He'd come here knowing full-well that he'd be seen and photographed. He'd stayed with me all night. He only left this morning because he had things to take care of, and I told him that I wanted to see my brother alone. I stood up and leaned over to kiss Aramis's forehead.

"Get some rest. I'll be back soon."

"Yep. Resting. Don't you worry, I'll be back to normal and partying in no time." Aramis winked and then cringed. "Fuck."

"Stop winking and stuff," I said.

"It's hard." He groaned.

"Elias says he wants you to go to the cottage in Roussillon when they discharge you so you can continue your healing."

"You've got to be kidding. They're going to banish me now for looking like this?" He raised his arm and gestured at his leg and face. "What? Does this not fit the narrative of what our family is supposed to look like?"

"It's not that, you idiot. He wants you to get one hundred percent better. You'll need physical therapy for your leg."

"I've broken a leg before. I'll live." He rolled his eyes.

"Stop being so stubborn. I'll see you soon." I walked out of the room and saw that Elias and Adeline were still with my mother. I walked over to them. "He's doing okay."

"We heard about Kayla," Elias said. "Why didn't you tell us?" He looked at Amir, who stood near the elevator. "I haven't addressed this with him yet, but I will."

"Don't. Don't get Amir in trouble for this. It was my fault for not making a big deal of it sooner. Do you think she slashed the tires or something?"

"How could Aramis have driven that far without noticing?" Adeline asked.

"If he'd been in any other car, it likely would have been impossible to do," Elias said. "But that one…" He shook his head. "Do you think she's capable of slashing your tires?"

"Yes."

"We need to have her arrested."

"Eli." Adeline grabbed his arm. "We can't just arrest her before we inspect the car."

"The hell, we can't. I'm the king, and my brother is in the hospital. My sister could have been killed." He yanked his arm away from Adeline.

"She's right, Eli." I licked my lips. "If you arrest her, it would be like

Father all over again. Your people will lose trust in you."

"I don't like knowing she's out there." He scowled.

"We'll have them inspect the tires immediately," Adeline said. "In the meantime, we have a public engagement and need to keep unrest at a minimum right now. "I'll be back later to visit with Aramis while you meet with Parliament."

We said our goodbyes and I stayed behind with my mother.

"It's such a shame," she said.

"What?"

"That you have to leave Benjamin because of his ex-girlfriend."

"What?" I said again and blinked. "I'm not going to leave him because of her. He has nothing to do with her anymore."

"Does she know that?"

"If she didn't before, she will now." I kissed my mother goodbye and walked over to Amir, ready to leave.

Chapter Twenty

Ben

I knew the media frenzy would be overwhelming, but I didn't anticipate how much. There were cameras everywhere, at all times. I was used to attention. It wasn't like I was the kind of man who could go to a pub with friends and not expect to be noticed, but I was still able to go out. These days, that seemed nearly impossible. I got Pilar though. I reminded myself of that. And they hadn't pried too much into my personal life, so that was nice. I knocked on the door again and waited with a sigh. When it opened, I smiled at my ex, Tamara, who was standing there wearing a large t-shirt and shorts.

"Well, if it isn't the newest member of the royal family." She opened the door wider. "Should I bow to you?"

"Don't be silly." I laughed, walking inside and looking around for a second before hearing little footsteps running full speed toward me. Then, I crouched and opened my arms as my son ran into them. I lifted him and turned as he laughed.

"Daddy, you were supposed to come earlier," he said as I set him back down.

"I wanted to, but I had some things to do." I ruffled his curly hair and smiled.

"Stay right here. I want to show you what I made in school." He ran off.

"Did you look into the football camp I sent you?" I looked at Tamara.

"I did. But, Ben, I have a million things going on right now. I haven't even properly moved in." She pointed at the boxes scattered around the living room.

"Tam, it's been two months."

"You try juggling moving with a four-year-old and a job."

"I told you I'd hire people to help you. You're too stubborn." I shook my head. "Where's the American, anyway?"

"The American's name is Jack," she said, rolling her eyes with a smile. "And you know very well that he's in New York for work. He's moving here at the end of next month."

"In here?" I raised my eyebrows.

"He's going to pay rent, don't worry."

"Hmm." I walked around. I'd gotten her this flat when I leased the one upstairs because I wanted to be close to my son. I hadn't anticipated what would happen if her boyfriend became more serious and actually wanted to move in with her. I guess that answered my question though.

"Ben, we talked about this." She sighed. "I told you I'd pay for this place, but you insisted."

"Tam, I don't care. I really don't." I turned to look at her.

Tamara was the closest I'd ever gotten to marriage. She was the relationship nobody knew about. I fucked it up by cheating on her with Kayla and regretted it every single day afterwards—not only because I missed out on my chance to be with a great woman, the mother of my child, but because I hurt her deeply, and she was one of the most caring people I knew. It had been a turbulent time for me, not that it was an excuse for doing what I'd done. Kayla had been there for me my entire life though, before, during, and after Tamara. My brother had just died from an overdose, I was alone in a big city with a million-dollar contract, and I was twenty-three years old. Back then, I'd been sorry I hurt Tamara, but not sorry I did it. I figured there was no way to stay faithful under those circumstances. I had been taught, by every man in my life, that it was okay to not stay faithful. Everything with Tamara was before I'd lived and seen things and met men who were decent and respectful to their significant others. These days, I regretted the hell out of all of it. To lose a woman like Tamara over someone like Kayla was just plain stupid, but if I was completely honest, Kayla sleeping around with my teammates was really what made me finally realize how much I had screwed up. Now, Tamara had Jack, the American, a great man who loved her fiercely. It helped that he was a fan of mine and also adored my son. In the beginning, it took me a while to embrace him, but seeing him with Asher was enough to sell me on the whole thing. So, him paying rent or not paying it was the last thing on my mind. If he was going to move in here with my son, I didn't need him to pay for anything.

"Jack isn't going to want a freebie anyway. He'll want to pay." She shot me a look as she started to wash dishes.

Asher ran back into the room, waving fistfuls of paper at me. I felt myself smile. I always smiled when around him. The kid made me happier than anyone else in my life.

"Look. I drew this and this." He showed me the first paper. It was a house with a family. There were four people drawn on the paper.

"Who are they?"

"You, Mommy, me, and Jack!"

"Ah." I chuckled, looking at Tam, who was watching me closely.

It was as if she half-expected me to flip out about her boyfriend half of the time. I didn't blame her. I'd been a different person when we were together, though I really hoped to show her that I was much calmer nowadays.

"I really love it." I cleared my throat and then looked at the rest of the artwork.

"I have to show you something else." He grabbed the papers from my hand and ran off again.

"He's non-stop," I said, shaking my head.

"You're telling me." Tamara turned the kitchen sink off and dried her hands. "So, what's going on with you and Princess Pilar? Is it serious?"

"I think so, but I don't know yet."

"You don't know yet?" She raised an eyebrow. "Do you want it to be serious."

"I do." There was no use denying it, but I hadn't spoken to Pilar about how she felt about it yet.

"Have you told her about Asher?"

"Not yet."

"You probably should."

"I will when the time is right. She has a lot on her mind right now."

"I'm sure she does. What happened to her and her brother was horrible, but you should consider telling her sooner rather than later."

"I know." I stood up and walked over to her. "I just don't want the paparazzi hounding you guys, and they will. The moment they find out about either of you, they won't leave you alone."

"They'd leave us alone if you're honest about us. Besides, we take some photos, sell them to a magazine directly, let the story run its course and be done with it." She shrugged.

"We agreed." I paused. "You were the one who told me you didn't want to be in the spotlight."

"I don't, but Ash is older now. I'm tired of playing dress-up every time we go out together. Or saying I'm your sister." She shot me a look.

"That was one time."

"One time too many, Ben." She rolled her eyes and continued organizing things in the kitchen. "Are you scared she'll like you less if you tell her?"

"No."

"Are you scared she won't like Ash?"

"No," I said vehemently. "Who wouldn't like him?"

"All I'm saying is, if you're really serious about her, you'll tell her. But then again, I thought you were serious about Sophia, and you never told her."

"Sophia and I were never serious."

"The media thought so."

"The media is full of lies. You of all people should know that."

"Does Pilar know about Kayla?"

"Yes." It was something I hated to discuss with Tam, of all people. "Kayla approached her while we were in Ibiza and again the day of the accident."

"Why was Kayla even in Ibiza? You invited her?"

"I had to."

"I will never understand how someone so smart can do so many stupid things." She rolled her eyes.

Thankfully, Asher ran back into the living room with some toys, and I busied myself playing with him. After bath time, I went back to my apartment, upstairs, away from the family I should be thrilled to have but had thrown away because of carelessness and selfishness. It was so the opposite of the version of myself I wanted Pilar to know, and I really wasn't sure I wanted to tell her anything at all.

Chapter Twenty-One

Pilar

Whoever thought it would be a good idea to charge me with working with children was borderline insane. I was not cut out for this. Yet, here I was, cutting paper with a group of five-year-olds who barely knew how to wipe themselves. One of them was eating his boogers, the little blonde named Saddie—*with an ie at the end*—was sitting prim and proper, legs crossed and head held high as if she were the princess at this table. And the last one, Marcus, was stabbing at the paper so hard, I was sure he'd cut himself by the end of this little exercise, safety scissors or not.

"Remember to cut along the dots," I said, my voice as chirpy as the forced smile on my face. "And please, Daniel, stop putting your hands in your mouth."

It was the only thing I could say to not mention the fact that I'd been watching him eat his boogers for the last five minutes. I sighed. Why did people have children on purpose? I didn't know. They were cute little rascals though, I'd give them that. And smart. Still. I couldn't imagine having these little germ carriers around me all the time. It was probably why I had been assigned to do this to begin with. Likely my mother's idea. She always said I needed to work on my maternal side because I had been born without an instinct. She wasn't wrong. I'd never cared for dogs or cats or birds or any other kind of pet. When our family dog, Shaggy, died when I was twelve, I didn't mourn for him the way the others did. Maybe I was broken. I bit my lip and chewed on that idea as I cut along the lines and folded the paper. We were making a row of hearts. Next, we had to color them. Saddie was already halfway there. I could tell she was a perfectionist, the way she made sure not to color outside the lines.

She was the girl I would have gotten along best with in school. I'd always liked everything to be neat and tidy in every aspect of my life. Until Ben. He made me want to give up all of those stupid pretenses. With him, I yearned to color outside the lines.

"Why are you blushing?" Saddie with the ie asked.

"Me? I'm not blushing."

"You are." She turned her nose up at me. "Are you thinking about Prince Charming?"

"Prince Charming?" I raised an eyebrow. "Definitely not."

"I think about Prince Charming a lot," she said. "You should too if you're going to marry one."

"I'm not certain I'll marry a prince."

"No?" she frowned. "But you're a princess. That's the best part."

"Is it, now?" I laughed. "I wasn't aware."

"What's the best part of being a princess?" Marcus sniffled, rubbing his nose with his hand. I watched where he put it next—on the scissors, of course.

"I guess doing things like this." I smiled.

"You mean cutting and coloring hearts for Miss Kate's classroom?" Daniel asked. "You don't have to be a princess to do that."

"True. But I meant spending time with smart kids like you."

"You don't have to be a princess to do that," Saddie said.

"So basically, the only cool thing about being a princess is finding and marrying a prince?" I asked.

"He's supposed to find you," Saddie said.

"Oh."

"He's supposed to rescue you from a tower," Marcus added.

"Oh?"

"And fight a dragon," Daniel said.

"Well, if I find myself sitting in a tower with a dragon guarding me, I'll be sure to call out for a prince. But I'll tell you what, my brother is a prince and I don't think he'd rescue anyone from a tower."

"No?" Saddie gasped. "What if the princess was in danger?"

"My best guess?" I leaned forward. "She'd have to save herself."

"Well, that's a boring story," Daniel said.

"Not romantic," Saddie added.

"But realistic." I shrugged. "We're the only ones who can save ourselves."

"But what about the dragon?" Marcus frowned.

"The dragon is life, and we are all the princesses and Prince Charmings."

"Hmm." That was Saddie. "I like my version better."

So do I, Saddie. So do I.

Chapter Twenty-Two

Pilar

My phone vibrated in my hand, and I smiled when I saw Ben's name on the screen. I answered.

"Hey."

"Hey." I could hear the smile in his voice. "I missed the sound of your voice."

I felt myself blush deeply. "Are you at practice?"

"I'm heading out now. Are you finished with your engagement?"

"Yes. I just got home about five minutes ago." I stretched my arms above my head with a yawn. "I don't know how teachers do it."

"That crazy, huh?"

"Crazier. Kids are a handful."

"Was it fun?"

"It was…" I paused. "Yeah, it actually was pretty fun once I got over the initial shock. I mean, I knew they'd be energetic, but it was a lot."

"I bet." He chuckled. "When can I see you again?"

"When do you want to see me again?"

"If it were up to me, I'd be seeing you right this second."

"Well, in that case, whenever you're free." My face hurt from smiling.

"In that case, I'll pick you up for dinner."

"In that case, I'll see you at seven."

He chuckled. "In that case, I can't wait to kiss you."

"Okay, I'm going to hang up now."

"See you soon."

* * * *

We went to a little sushi restaurant near my building. It was usually quiet and not too crowded, but even so, Amir and the rest of the security went ahead and made sure they could accommodate Ben and me in the back, away from prying eyes. I wondered how often he had this issue and if he ventured out much. Once we were seated across from each other at a table so small we were forced to touch each other, even if we wanted to keep our hands and legs to ourselves, I let out a breath and smiled at him. The table was on the floor, so we had to take our shoes off to sit, and it was inside of what felt like a little room with a curtain for doors, but we couldn't see anyone, and no one could see us.

"Do you venture out often?" I asked. "I mean, nightclubs aside."

"Generally not in the city."

"Why is that? You don't like to be photographed unless it's staged?" I was half-joking, but he nodded.

"What? Really?" I leaned in just as the server set down two cups of water between us. "I would have never guessed that."

"Why? Do you look for photographs of me often?"

"Maybe."

"Maybe," he repeated, taking a sip of his water. "I guess I'm flattered."

"You guess?"

"Sure. I mean, a beautiful princess looking for photos of me. How could I not be flattered?" He winked as he set the cup down. I felt myself blush.

"I have a question. Why didn't you ever try to talk to me at my mother's Sunday dinners?"

"I always spoke to you at those."

"To be nice. And because you knew I liked you." I swore my blush was getting deeper, which was dumb considering we were already together.

"I always liked you."

"So why not ask me out?"

"You had a boyfriend, remember?"

"We saw each other a lot after he and I broke up." I raised an eyebrow.

"Well, then, let's just say I had my reasons, and I don't want to disclose them at the moment." He winked. "I'm a firm believer in that everything happens for a reason. I think it took seeing you in Ibiza for me to finally make my move, so I'm glad you were there."

"Me too. I mean, despite the fact that the night you took me home I was completely blacked out."

"The first night I took you home." He smiled. "I fully plan on taking you home tonight. To my real home."

"Word on the street is you rarely take women to your house. Should I be flattered?"

"Word on the street." He laughed. "I didn't realize my personal life was discussed at such length."

"Oh, it is. You're always the topic of conversation when you're in the room."

"I'm glad I didn't know that."

"Why? Would it have gone to your head?"

"No, it would have made me a little more self-conscious."

"Really?" My eyes widened. "You?"

"Yeah, and it would have probably gone to my head." He chuckled, his eyes darkening as he looked over at me. "You know what I really want to discuss?"

"What?" My chest seemed to constrict with the way he stared at me.

"What you're wearing right now." His eyes trailed down the short black dress and large diamond mesh fishnets I wore, and his hand slid over to my knee, grazing each hole in the stockings. "This is driving me crazy."

"Yeah?" I whispered, licking my lips, wishing he'd never stop looking at me or touching me.

"Yeah." He bit his lower lip as if he were in pain as he continued touching my leg. "I can't stop thinking about fucking you on this table, on this floor, on the pillows we're sitting on."

"Oh God." I was already panting. "We're in public."

"Well then, I guess it would serve no purpose for me to ask you to wait two seconds and then stand up and sit on this table right here, in front of me, with your legs spread." He licked his lips again, and I swore I could practically feel that tongue against me, between my legs.

"I'd do it." I shivered. "But what are you going to do in those two seconds?"

"Make sure no one will bother us for the next half hour."

"Oh."

He stood and walked outside, shutting the curtains behind him. I could hear his voice but couldn't make out what he was saying. I thought about that photograph someone had sold of me standing on the balcony in Ibiza and wondered if this was a mistake. Would someone walk in here without permission and snap a photo? Would I care? I stood up and did as he'd instructed. I didn't care. I also trusted Ben implicitly and knew he wouldn't let that happen.

As I sat there, waiting for him to return, I wondered if he'd done this before. He'd said he normally went out of town unless he didn't mind being photographed, but that didn't mean he hadn't taken women on secret dates and done this with them. I hated the way my heart cracked at the mere thought. Here I'd always thought I wasn't a jealous person, but when it came to Ben, it seemed that everything bothered me. Well, everything that had to do with him having a normal life before me. Maybe it was because I couldn't help but think of what his life would be like after me, and I absolutely hated the thought of not having him in *my* life.

I heard him behind me as I sat on the low table, waiting. My legs were only slightly parted, but they were separated enough. The room was dim, so he wouldn't be able to see that I wasn't wearing any panties under the fishnets. He wouldn't be able to make out much of anything, but I knew he'd feel it. He settled himself between my legs as if he were sitting in front of a plate. I hoped he'd treat me like the meal he'd come here for.

When his hands closed around my ankles before letting go and moving upward, I knew he would. My chest began to rise and fall with my breaths. With every inch of me he touched, it seemed as if he took my breath away a little more. My lungs felt as if they were preparing for an onslaught. His dark gaze met mine beneath long lashes, and I felt like I might explode right then. When I felt his fingers reach the inside of my thighs, my head fell back.

"No panties?" He tsked. "What a naughty princess." His fingers inched closer to where I needed them. "Were you hoping I'd find out?"

I bit my lip hard, bringing my head up to meet his gaze, then nodded.

"Were you hoping I'd rip these stockings off?" He raised an eyebrow. I nodded again. "Interesting."

"Please, Ben." It was a plea.

"Please what, Princess?"

"Please touch me, do something."

"Oh, I fully intend to." He brought his mouth down to my calf and bit me. "But you need to promise you'll be quiet."

"I will be." I nodded quickly. The restaurant was loud, but I knew people surrounded us, and they'd hear me if I wasn't quiet.

"And you have to promise not to let me rip these stockings." He bit my other calf. "I quite like them."

"You can rip them. I don't care." The large holes were everywhere, including the crotch. But even if he didn't rip them, he'd definitely stretch them to the point of no return if he continued this way. Honestly, I didn't mind one bit.

"Oh, no, Princess. I'll care. I want these intact."

"But...but how will you...?"

"We'll just have to find a way." Both of his thumbs slid inside of me at once, and I dropped my head back with a moan. "Quiet, Princess."

"Yes," I whispered, my hips moving, grinding against his fingers. I'd never thought I'd feel this needy, at least not before him, but I felt like I would explode if he didn't do more. I felt like I might die if he did.

"Did you think about me often before this started, Princess?"

"Hmm." I nodded, gasping when more fingers joined the thumbs in his ministrations. Now, he was inside of me and on my clit, stroking and rubbing circles. I wouldn't survive this. I wouldn't.

"Did you touch yourself?"

"Yes."

"Did you close your eyes when you were fucking your ex and pretend it was me between your legs?"

I gasped loudly, opening my eyes to meet his. I nodded, the shame of my admission coloring my face, but I couldn't seem to care. When he flashed that wolfish grin of his, I definitely didn't.

"Good." He took his hands away, and just before I opened my mouth to complain, he replaced them with his face, his tongue, sucking me, licking me, biting me.

There was absolutely no way for me to stay quiet. No way. He wasn't playing fair, and he knew it. My hands flew to his hair, and I gripped his curls hard, tugging at him to stop, to keep going, I wasn't sure. Either way, he didn't listen. He continued feasting on me, eating me as if I were his appetizer, entree, and dessert. I came hard. Loudly. My shouts were muffled by the hand he shot up to my face to cover my mouth. I'd never been more turned on in my entire life.

He pulled away, rocking back on his heels as he looked at me, his mouth glistening with evidence of what he'd just done. I watched, wordlessly, as he lowered his trousers and slid on a condom. I licked my lips reflexively, wishing I had the energy to get up and take him into my mouth, but also knowing that if I didn't, he'd fuck me, and I wasn't sure which outcome I wanted more. I opted to stay put. He spread my legs more and brought a hand between us. I felt his fingers stroking my clit again and instantly began to move, my body reawakened by his touch. He didn't leave his fingers there for long.

"I need to make room in these stockings," he said, his voice rough as he settled between my legs. "I need to make room in this little pussy for me."

"Yes," I gasped, arching my back and biting my lip hard as he slid inside of me, inch by inch. My eyes shut, and my head flew back, and I moaned out, "Ben," as he filled me. "Yes, Ben. Yes."

"Say it again, Princess." He slid out and pushed all the way in again.

"Ben."

"Yes," he hissed. "Yes. You're fucking perfect for me. Perfect."

It felt as if he were saying so much more than those words, but I had no time to question him because he really started to fuck me then, and nothing else mattered in that moment.

Chapter Twenty-Three

Ben

"Have you read this?" David dropped the newspaper onto the kitchen counter.

"No, I read the news like a normal person—online." I went back to the sandwich I had been making for Asher.

"Well, this is the kind of news that makes headlines in the actual papers," he said. "Which means, it's big."

"What's the news?"

"Kayla is talking about writing a tell-all about the time she spent with you."

"What?" I laughed then stopped when I saw the serious expression on David's face. "You're full of shit."

"I'm not." He picked up the paper again and opened it, walking over to me as he tipped it for me to see the headline. It read: *Golden Boy Benjamin Drake's Rusty Past.*

"Why would they give her this kind of attention?" I yanked the paper from his hand and read the words beneath the headline.

"Maybe because you're such a mystery to them," David suggested.

"Jesus Christ, David. You're supposed to make sure this kind of shit doesn't happen." I slammed the paper down. "What about Asher? Did she say anything about him?"

"Not yet, but my guess is that will be part of the tell-all. You should have had her sign an NDA."

"When? When I was fourteen years old and living with my fucking parents? When I was dealing with my brother Ezra's death? When was I going to make her sign this NDA? I just found out what an NDA is a few years ago!" I threw up my hands and started pacing the kitchen.

"Is everything okay, Daddy?" Asher ran into the kitchen. "Is my sandwich done? My tummy is hungry."

"Yes, buddy. Everything's fine." I took a deep breath and let it out, picking up his plate and setting it down on the small table where he liked to sit. "I put pastrami in it, just like you like."

"Mommy always puts pastrami." He took a bite. "And salami."

"Well, your mother has me beat once again." I winked at him, then turned to David and whispered, "Tamara is going to kill me."

"She's going to kill me too." David took out his phone. "I'm going to call Idris."

"You haven't called him? Isn't the lawyer the first person you should call when you see something like this?" I paused. "Shit. I have to tell Pilar."

"I'm sure she already knows about it."

"All the more reason I should call her." I picked up the phone and dialed. "I have practice at three today. You'll take Asher to the playground while I'm there?" I looked at David.

"Of course." He smiled at Ash. "We're going to the museum. Right, buddy?"

"Yes, and we're going for ice cream."

"Not too much ice cream," I warned.

"What's too much ice cream?" Pilar asked in my ear, startling me. I walked out of the kitchen to find a quiet spot. "Nothing. I was talking to David. So, have you seen the news?"

"How could I not?"

"And?"

"And what?" she waited.

"How do you feel about it?"

"I think she's crazy, and you need to do some serious damage control before it gets out of hand."

"I'm not asking you for public relations advice, Pilar. I asked how you felt about it."

She was quiet for a moment. When she spoke again, her voice was almost a whisper, "I don't love it."

"Why?" I held my breath. Why was I asking and feeling as if my life depended on the answer she gave?

"For starters, I know this can't be easy for you. You've done such a good job of keeping most of your personal life out of the limelight. I didn't even know you had a brother before I met you. And, well, I don't like that she has so much insight to begin with." She was quiet for a long moment. "I'm jealous."

"You have nothing to be jealous about," I said but couldn't help my smile.

"I feel like I don't know you, not like she does."

"You do know me. I want you to know me." I sighed, suddenly wishing we were having this conversation face-to-face. "Come by the arena later. I have practice at three, but we can do something afterwards."

"Will I get to watch you practice?"

"Do you want to watch me?"

"I would kill to watch you practice," she said, a squeak in her voice. I laughed.

"Come by a little before three. I'll let security know to be on the lookout for a very important fan."

"Number one fan, you mean."

"You're my number one fan?"

"Of course, I am."

I was smiling so hard, my face hurt. Jesus, I felt like a kid again. I looked over at Asher, who was finishing his lunch. I knew he would come running soon. I needed to tell Pilar about him. I would later today. We hung up, and I spent the rest of my afternoon with Asher until I needed to head to the arena for practice.

Chapter Twenty-Four

Pilar

When Amir and I pulled up to the arena, I was practically bouncing in the passenger seat. He looked over as he put the car in park.

"I hope you're going to at least try to play it cool in there." His eyes twinkled. "Because you sure are acting like one of those kids at the school the other day."

"Amir." I reached over and grabbed his forearm, squeezing it as I spoke. "We are about to watch Le Bleus practice. In real life. On the pitch. In front of us. Without a million other people in the stadium."

"I got that." He laughed. "Because you're dating one of the players. You *are* dating, right?"

I thought about how to answer that as we got out of the car and met in front of it.

"I mean, we go on dates." I smiled. I couldn't seem to stop smiling.

"I like seeing you like this." Amir grinned at me as we walked. "You're lighter. More fun."

"More fun?" I gasped, laughing. "Are you saying I was boring before I started dating Ben? Is it because we weren't able to do things like this?"

"You know that's not what I meant, but this is definitely a perk." We slowed when we reached the second security gate, and he walked ahead. "Let me see where we're supposed to go."

"I'll be here." I looked around the stadium, refraining from jumping up and down only because I knew there were cameras everywhere, and I didn't want to look like a fool on video.

I started walking down the sidewalk, looking at the plaques on the wall, reading about past players and the team's record.

"Impressive, isn't it?" The voice startled me, and I was even more surprised to see it was Kayla. So taken aback that I couldn't even think of words. She smiled, seemingly amused by my reaction.

"What are you doing here?"

"Picking up some things I left at someone's house." She lifted the Le Bleu duffel bag in her hand for me to focus on. "Has Ben taken you to his place? Probably not, right?"

"That's none of your business." My ears were ringing.

I wondered where Amir was. We hadn't yet filed a restraining order against Kayla, but seeing her here made me want to. We still hadn't gotten proof of what had happened with the accident. The car had been taken to the pound and logged as a total loss with the insurance company.

"I can't say I blame him for not taking you," she said. "He likes to keep things hidden from the women he dates."

"I don't know what the point of all of this is. If it's to scare me away from Ben, it won't work. We're adults, and we do as we please."

"Of course." She shrugged. "You're probably only looking for a casual relationship."

But I wasn't, was I? I hated the way her words seemed to seep into my brain and marinate. And stew they would. I knew, and she seemed to know it as well.

"Don't you have a book to write?" I asked. "Your claim to fame."

"I never said I was going to write one. I said I *could* write one with all the things I know about him. The papers twisted my words."

"I'm sure they did." I stared at her.

She was really pretty, in an unassuming, fresh-faced way that might have made me feel slightly uncomfortable had it not been for the fact that I knew Ben didn't want her.

"So, I'll get out of your hair now," she said, smiling. "Tell Ben I'll see him when he's finished exploring this…whatever he thinks this thing is with you. As if a princess would ever truly fall for a man from the other side of the tracks."

"It doesn't matter what side of the tracks he's from. It matters what side he's on now, and last time I checked, he was on mine." I flashed her a smile. "But if you want to wait for him to go back to yours, be my guest."

"Tell yourself whatever you want, Princess. It doesn't change the fact that it's not me or you he'll choose. The two of us are distractions. I just happen to be a long-term one. But I know my place, and soon, you'll know yours." She walked away without another word, and I was left wondering what she meant by all of that.

"Is everything okay?" Amir asked from behind me. I jumped and turned to him. "I was here the whole time. I just didn't want to overstep. You seemed like you had it handled."

"Until she threw that last curveball." I gnawed my bottom lip for a second before taking a deep breath and reminding myself of who I was and *where* I was. "But yes, I'm okay. Do we still not have news on the tires?"

"Not yet." He looked at me. "I know you don't want to make a big deal out of this because you think she'll run to the papers if you place a restraining order against her, but I think it's necessary. It's getting out of hand."

"I think you're right."

We started walking toward the entrance of the arena. Amir turned to me. "So, what does that saying mean? Threw a curveball? Is that an American thing?"

"I have no idea. Adeline says it all the time, and now I can't seem to get rid of it." I frowned, thinking about it. "I think it has to do with baseball."

"Baseball? Who watches baseball?"

"Americans." I felt myself smile. "And Adeline."

"Interesting."

We walked through the gates and into the section of the stadium where the lockers and suites were. The security guard escorting us pointed at things as we walked, giving us a tour of sorts. I tried really hard to pay attention, but I was too amazed at being here and walking these halls to wrap my head around any of the fun facts. He took us to the locker rooms, which were empty since the guys were on the field, but he couldn't let us go inside because of that. We saw the suites, the dining hall, and the seating areas that only people with connections to the team and the media were allowed in. I knew my brothers had been in here with their friends, but of course I'd never been invited. It wasn't like I'd ever asked to come. If I had, they would have brought me along. As we walked out toward the field, I felt the adrenaline pumping through me as if I were the one who was about to run out onto the pitch.

"Do you see him?" Amir asked as we looked at the team, running back and forth on the field. When Ben caught my eye, I pointed and jumped up.

"There!" I laughed and turned to Amir. "Take a picture of me. I have to send it to Eli and Aramis."

When he gave me my phone back, I sent the picture and typed: *I'm pretty sure I have the best seats in the house.*

Aramis: NO WAY

Eli: WHY DIDN'T YOU INVITE US?

Me: You never invite me when you come. So there.

Eli: Not fair

Aramis: Tell Ben we're no longer friends

I laughed as I read their responses aloud to Amir, who laughed along with me. When Ben was finished playing, he introduced me to some of his friends. I'd already met Alex in Ibiza, but I was giddy at meeting the rest of them, not only because I was a fan, but because Ben was obviously making it clear that this wasn't temporary.

Chapter Twenty-Five

Pilar

I loved being in his house. Everything about it was so…him, from the neutral walls to the library filled with memorabilia and trophies he'd won. I'd caught a quick glimpse of his bedroom during the tour he gave me, but our food arrived before I could explore much else. Now, we were on the floor around his coffee table, having sushi and drinking wine. It was the most glorious date I'd ever had.

"Are you in pain?" I watched as he finished chewing the roll of sushi he'd just put into his mouth.

"Do you mean am I sore?"

"Yes. I'm sore just from watching your drills today."

"I think I've forgotten what not being sore feels like." He chuckled. "I've been playing since I was three. I guess I'm just conditioned to it."

"That's pretty amazing." His stamina was pretty amazing too. I felt myself blush as the thought crossed my mind and tried to hide it by looking away, but Ben reached for my hand. I couldn't help but meet his gaze, which was slightly amused, a bit turned on.

"What are you thinking about?"

"How much I want you."

"Ah." He chuckled lightly as he brought my hand to his lips and nipped my thumb. "That's a nice thing to think about."

"I also can't help but think that you're much more experienced than I am." I fought to keep my gaze on his.

"You're perfect." He tugged my arm and pulled me closer to him, searching my eyes. "Hey, you're perfect. I couldn't imagine a more ideal woman."

His hands grazed my torso as he pushed them under my shirt, stopping at the elastic of my bra.

"Is this okay?" he whispered against my neck, breathing me in as he kissed me.

"More than okay." I pushed out my chest, inviting him to do more.

He didn't work his hands under my bra the way I thought he might. Instead, he brought his hands behind me, unsnapping the clasp. Ben pulled back and looked into my eyes. There was so much more than lust in them, and I didn't know what that meant. Regardless, my heart galloped with such force that I thought he might hear it. Bringing my hand up to touch his face, I caressed his jaw, the five o'clock shadow tickling the tips of my fingers. Even as I touched him, I couldn't quite believe that I was with him, with the man I'd crushed on for years and pictured doing this with more times than I cared to admit. He watched me for a long while, his hands still just under my breasts as he seemingly savored my hands on his face.

"You're entirely too beautiful for me," he said, and the way he looked at me made me believe it.

"You're entirely too handsome for me." I smiled, leaning into him and kissing his lips.

I gasped as he brought his fingers to my jaw and deepened the kiss, his tongue dancing with mine, his erection pressing into my pussy so hard through our clothes that I had no control over myself when my body began to move, seeking the pleasure he promised. His hands finally cupped both of my breasts, his fingers pinching my nipples so hard I had to stop kissing him and throw my head back to moan. He pinched them again, his hands quickly working to rid me of my shirt and bra for his mouth to latch on to each of them, nuzzling, kissing, sucking. With his lips, his hands, he made me feel a sense of abandon I'd never experienced before. He brought out a sexually starved version of me I hadn't even known was in there.

I continued moving against his cock, even though we were still both wearing jeans and I knew I wouldn't find the release I needed. As if reading my thoughts, Ben pulled away. Suddenly we were both standing, rapidly taking off the rest of our clothes. He brought me back to his lap with me straddling him and continued marking my skin with his lips. His hand moved south, his gentle nips turning to bites as his fingers began moving against me.

"You're so wet, Princess." He groaned against my chest. "Have you been this wet all along?"

"Y-yes," I stammered. I wished my body would stop grinding, but I knew I was absolutely unable to contain myself at this point.

"I need a condom," he breathed. "I want to fuck you like this. I want you to ride my cock with that wet pussy."

"Oh God." I threw back my head. This was unlike anything else I'd ever done. The dirty talk, the naughty things. Every time I was with Ben, he brought something to the table that I hadn't known I was missing, and I knew I'd never be the same. Because of him.

"Reach for the condom. Back pocket of my jeans." He leaned in, his tongue swirling on my left nipple.

I reached for the pocket in his pants on the floor, not without hardship. My entire body was vibrating now. His fingers were inside my pussy and sliding against my clit, his tongue on my nipple as his other hand worked the other breast. I was sure I'd die from overstimulation. Somehow, I managed to retrieve and open the condom.

"Slide it on me, Princess." His voice was gruff, and even gruffer when I did as I was told. "Such a good girl. Yes."

I wasn't going to survive Ben Drake. There was absolutely no chance of it. I knew that now more than ever. Not when he could touch me like this and make me feel this way.

"Ride me, baby." He grabbed my hips and settled me over him, sliding me down ever so slowly, inch by inch. My breath lodged in my lungs as he filled me. He was huge, but somehow, my body welcomed him. "Ride me, Princess. Ride me."

So, I did.

"Fuck," I said, my heart in my throat as I moved on top of him. "Oh my Gggggggggod."

"Yes. Yes. Yes," he chanted. "Pilar. Fuck me, Pilar."

Spurred on by his pleas and the way everything inside of me seemed to vibrate, I rode him hard and fast, my nails digging into his strong shoulder blades as his fingers dug into my hips, my ass, any part of me he could reach and use to control the tempo. I threw my head back, feeling another orgasm build from deep inside me and gripped him so hard I was sure I'd draw blood.

As I reached ecstasy, I shouted his name and kept on shouting as he yelled mine and pumped into me harder than before. I shook and vibrated against him as my eyes closed, then I felt him kiss the top of my head as he whispered, "So perfect for me."

* * * *

I was trying to be quiet as I walked out of his flat and shut the door behind me, but I gasped loudly when I turned around and found a woman and a little boy standing there.

"Hi." I frowned, confused. This floor housed only Ben's apartment, and he was asleep.

"Hi." The woman smiled, a kind expression that reached her blue eyes. "Is Ben in there?"

"He's sleeping." I felt my frown deepen. "He told me the door locks as soon as it shuts."

"That's okay." She wiggled the key in her hand. "I have a key."

"Oh." I moved to walk away from the door, still looking at her. "Are you family?"

"I guess." She laughed. "If girlfriends are considered family."

"And sons," the little boy said, speaking for the first time since I'd seen them.

"G-g-girlfriend and son?"

"Ex-girlfriend," she corrected. "We are definitely not together anymore."

"But he is…his…son." I was stuttering, but I couldn't wrap my head around what I was hearing.

"He hasn't told you," she said, and she sounded as heartbroken as I felt. I shook my head, blinking back the tears I felt coming on.

I didn't care that Ben had a son or a serious ex-girlfriend. I just couldn't understand how he could keep those things from me. They seemed like the sorts of things someone would reveal on a first date, or a second, maybe even a third. We'd spent so much time together. Nearly every waking moment together in Ibiza and here since we'd gotten back. My heart felt as if it might beat out of my chest.

"I'm sorry," the woman said. "Truly. I am. I thought he'd said something. If he brought you here."

"He didn't." I wiped the tear that trickled down my cheek and smiled at the little boy, who looked just like his father—brown curls, caramel skin, green eyes. "It was so nice to meet you both."

I walked away and into the elevator. The minute the doors closed, I started to cry.

Chapter Twenty-Six

Pilar

On top of everything else that had fallen upon me, we'd just received confirmation that two of my four tires had been slashed before the accident. There were no longer any lingering doubts in my mind. I knew for certain that Kayla had been behind it. Would there be a way to prove it? I didn't know. What I did know was that I wanted her arrested for it. I wasn't a vindictive person, but my brother was still recovering from the accident. Aramis could have died. *I* could have died had I been driving. My lower lip quivered at the thought of it. When my phone rang again and I saw Ben's name on the screen accompanied by a picture of us together on the balcony in Ibiza, I thought I might lose it all over again.

"You can't just ignore his calls forever," Joss said.

"I don't understand how we didn't know he had a son. The only thing I found on him was his brother's death. I thought that was awful, but this…" Adeline said in a whisper. She glanced at Elias. "Did you know?"

"No." Elias looked at Aramis, whose face fell as he nodded.

"I knew." Aramis shut his eyes briefly as we all stared at him. "In my defense, Ben told me when we were both out of our minds, wasted. We had a heart-to-heart about it, and I didn't give it much thought afterwards. I never met the kid. I just figured he didn't want him around me because I was always flanked by photographers when we were together. My guess is that he doesn't want his son in the spotlight."

"Obviously." Joss rolled her eyes. "That doesn't excuse him from not telling Pilar about him though."

"I thought you two were casual," Aramis said.

"We are. We were," I snapped. I swore my brother could get on my nerves faster than anyone. "That doesn't mean I like being lied to."

"Did he lie though?" Elias asked.

"I seriously cannot stand either of you right now. I was trying to make this a girls' night, and you two invited yourselves over. As if anyone wanted you here. And you're really annoying me."

"The only reason you wanted to make it a girls' night was so you could have people to commiserate with." Aramis raised an eyebrow. "Since girls are haters."

"We are not," Joss jumped in.

"No?" He shot her a look. "You hate on me all day, every day."

"That's because you're arrogant and annoying." She took a deep breath. "And honestly, I don't know how I'm going to play matchmaker and find someone who will actually want to put up with you."

Aramis bit his lip as he looked at Joss, but no amount of lip biting could ever keep him from speaking his mind. So I braced myself when I saw him open his mouth. "You sure it's not because you'd rather be the one warming my bed?"

"Oh my God." Joss blushed as she stood up and stomped over to the door, glancing at him before walking out. "I can't stand you."

Aramis laughed loudly as the door slammed behind her.

"You're such a jerk," I said.

"She's too easy to rile up." He grinned momentarily before turning his attention to Elias. "See? No one wants to be responsible for this matchmaking idea of yours."

"Well, she will be responsible for it, and you will settle down even if it's just for pretenses," Elias said. "You're supposed to be giving yourself time to heal. You've only been out of the hospital for two weeks and the only thing you've done with that time is get piss drunk and sleep around more than you ever have."

"No more than I have before," Aramis argued.

"Can we get back to the issue at hand?" I slammed my hand on the side table. "The man I'm dating has a son that I didn't know about, and I don't know what to do with that information."

"Maybe speak to him about it," Adeline suggested.

"He should have spoken to me about it already."

"I agree, but I'm sure he had his reasons for not doing so."

"Maybe he doesn't trust me." The thought brought tears to my eyes.

"Just give him time," Elias said. "We're not exactly known to be the most forthcoming family."

"But I am. I was. I've always been honest with him."

"So, talk to him. Hear him out," Aramis suggested. "You'll see him on Sunday anyway."

My shoulders slumped. Sunday would be the first Sunday dinner in a long time. Elias and Adeline were taking over for my mother. She hadn't wanted to host them since my father passed away, which was understandable. Still, Adeline and Elias thought it was important to keep it going, and I understood that. Sunday dinners had become modern-day Court, where we invited old friends and new to share food and drinks with. It was so much fun and was the one place I could sneak glances at Benjamin Drake for hours without him noticing. Now, having him in the same room felt suffocating. A child. He had a child with someone. The only reason I'd been able to get this far with him was by ignoring the fact that he had a colorful past, but a child made that impossible to ignore. And the boy was adorable and looked like a carbon copy of his father. Still. A child. I still thought of myself as a child. I couldn't even pretend to think I'd be a good stepmother to one. I grabbed my purse and stood.

"Where are you going?" Aramis asked.

"Out. I need to think, and this little meeting is doing nothing for me."

"See you Sunday." Aramis gave me a hug and cringed when I did the same. I let go quickly.

"I'm sorry. I keep forgetting."

"I don't." He shot a look at Elias. "But when I drink, it's tolerable."

"You need to figure out healthier ways to deal with your pain," Adeline said, raising an eyebrow. "Like yoga."

"Yoga." Aramis scoffed.

"She's not wrong." I put my hand to my mouth and blew a kiss at the room. "See you Sunday."

"Pilar," Elias called out. I turned to face him again. "We're having her arrested tonight. Quietly. We'll question her and go from there."

"You mean the police will question her," Adeline said, raising an eyebrow. "You're not going to be present for that, Eli."

"We'll see."

"She's right, brother. You want all of us to play our part in pretending we're just one big, happy, non-dysfunctional, family, then you need to play your part as well and let the police do their job without your meddling." That was Aramis. Surprisingly.

"I want justice," Eli said.

"So do I," I said. "I'm sure Aramis wants that, too. But let them do their jobs."

With that, I left.

Chapter Twenty-Seven

Ben

It was day two of no communication with Pilar, and I didn't like it. I still had practice and Asher with me while Tamara helped Jack move into her apartment. I thought about showing up at her place, but I would have to take Asher with me, and I wasn't sure how we'd be received. The last thing I wanted was for either of them to be put in an awkward position. Well, it couldn't be more awkward than what Tamara had explained to me. She'd said that Pilar had tears in her eyes. It made me feel awful, only made worse by the fact that she wouldn't answer my calls or texts now. I glanced at my phone again just in case. Still nothing. My living room looked catastrophic—toys were everywhere. Asher and I had gone from racing mini cars, to playing cards, to drawing, and now putting together a puzzle. Typically, David's OCD-driven self was here, picking up as we went, but since I'd given him the day off, it was just Asher and I and the pizza we would order in later.

"Is it true she's a princess?" Asher asked.

I blinked up from the puzzle piece in my hand. "What?"

"The lady we saw the other day leaving your flat. Mommy said she's a princess."

"She is a princess."

"Wow." His eyes widened before narrowing. "She didn't have a princess dress on though."

"She didn't, but she's definitely a princess."

"Does she live in a castle?"

"No," I answered slowly. This was surely not going to help me prove my point. "But her brother, the king, does."

I didn't bother to explain that Elias didn't actually live in the castle. He was supposed to. He should, but he only took his appointments there. He slept in a private residence that was as big as a castle, so I guess it didn't matter that it wasn't the castle everyone wanted to believe he slept in.

"Her brother is the king?" Asher shouted. "Like a real king?"

"Yes." I bit my lip to contain my laughter. An excited Asher was always adorable.

"Do you know him?"

"Yes."

"Can I meet him?"

"Sure."

"You don't sound sure." He walked up to where I was on the floor in front of the puzzle we'd been building for the better part of an hour and sat on my lap. He put his arms around my neck and squeezed. "You look sad."

"Not anymore. Your hugs make me instantly happy." I kissed his head. He squeezed me harder.

"Does the princess make you happy?"

"She does." I felt myself smile.

"Am I going to see her again?"

"Maybe. I hope so, buddy." I exhaled, ruffling his curls as I leaned against the sofa behind me. "She's a little bit sad right now too."

"Does she have kids?"

"No."

"Maybe I should give her a hug too then."

"Maybe." I smiled wider and pulled him against my chest. "I'm so lucky to have you."

"I know." He yawned.

I closed my eyes, and we both fell asleep right there on the floor in the midst of the chaos.

Chapter Twenty-Eight

Pilar

More than anything, I wished Kayla would stop talking to the press. It seemed she'd tapered off after she made her initial announcements, but nope. That was wishful thinking. Now every single tabloid had her face on the cover. What was worse, it was her face *and* Ben's. Some of the photos she'd sold were of the two of them kissing and holding hands. Even though he looked very young in them, which helped to prove that he wasn't lying about them not being together, it didn't make it any less hurtful to see him with another woman. Kissing her. Holding hands with her. I reminded myself about the child and sighed heavily.

"You need to stop looking at these." Joss shook her head as she walked over to my bed and began collecting the tabloids. "Who brings you this crap anyway?"

"Amir." I shut my eyes and fell onto my pillow.

"Why would he——?"

"Because I told him he had to." I sat up quickly. "I want to know what people are saying about all of this. There are photos of me with Ben, and then Ben with Kayla and I just…" I sighed again. "I don't know what to think anymore."

"You know what's odd?" Joss sat down on the edge of my bed. "There are no photos of his ex or the boy. Anywhere. Not even Kayla has mentioned them."

"I know. I found it odd as well."

"It's weird."

"I agree. I just wish he'd trusted me with the news. I wouldn't have gone to the tabloids with it." My voice weakened. "I can't believe he didn't tell me."

"Have you given him a chance to explain himself?"

"No." I shook my head slowly. "I don't think I can hear his voice or see him without crying."

"Okay, let's talk about this." She stood and walked over to me, sitting down beside me. "What exactly bothers you? Is it the fact that he didn't tell you, or that he has a child with someone else?"

"Both." My voice broke. "Both. It's so dumb. The boy is like five, and it's not like I ever thought I'd get together with Ben. I dreamed of it, yes, but I didn't think it would happen, and now I find out he has this experience with another woman. This life-bonding thing. She'll always be in his life."

"As she should be, P." Joss set her hand on mine. "That's a good thing. It means he's a good, decent human being."

I wiped my face. "I hadn't thought of it like that."

"Well, you should. He's a good man, that one. And he really likes you, P. The man of your dreams. Heck, of all of our dreams. And he likes you." She emphasized that last part. I grabbed a pillow and threw it at her.

"He better not be in your dreams any longer."

"Only sometimes." She put her hands up. I threw another pillow at her. She laughed. "I'm just joking." She stood up.

"Joking about what?" Aramis asked, walking into my bedroom. He had a black walking cast on now that he flaunted as if it were the Pope's bloody shoe.

"Does no one knock?" I rolled my eyes, exhaling.

"What are we joking about? I'm up for jokes today." He walked over to my bed and sat down on the edge.

"Joss was saying that she still dreams about Ben," I said.

"Still dreams about Ben?" Aramis's eyebrow rose. "You dreamed about him in the past?"

"All the time," Joss said, winking at me so I knew she was joking. She walked toward the door.

"And what happened in these dreams?" Aramis asked.

"Dirty things," she said.

His expression darkened. "Really?"

"You asked." She shrugged a shoulder and walked out.

"It's true," I said. "You asked."

He shrugged both shoulders and stared off into the distance, the way he did when he was sulking. Something he was always doing when Joslyn was involved, whether he knew it or not.

"What are you doing here anyway?" I cleared my throat.

"I was in the area, so I figured I'd check on you."

"Shouldn't I be the one checking on you?"

"I just left my physical therapist." He smiled. "I'm fine."

"How are your burns?"

"There." His lips flattened. "I don't think they're something I'll ever get used to, but who knows. Maybe it'll be like tattoos. People get used to those."

I didn't bother mentioning that he'd never wanted tattoos because he was always particular about marking his perfect skin. His words. I scooted over and gently put my arms around him.

"I love you, Aramis."

"I love you, sis." He laid his head on my arm. "Have you spoken to Ben yet?"

"No." I pulled away and looked at him. "I know it's dumb, but I can't get over it."

"You're going to see him soon."

"I know."

"I don't even know what to say about this, to be honest. I never saw you together. What I do know is that he's a great friend, and he's been asking non-stop about you." He shot me a look. "The man doesn't ask about anyone, Pilar."

"Like you said, he's a great friend of yours. Of course, he's going to ask you about me."

"He may be a great friend, P, but Ben's a free spirit when it comes to women. He's a take-'em-or-leave-'em kind of guy. He doesn't sit around sulking, and he's definitely sulking now, whether he knows it or not."

"Sounds familiar." I raised an eyebrow.

"What is that supposed to mean?" He frowned.

"You sit around sulking every time Joss even mentions a new guy."

"That is..." He started shaking his head and rolling his eyes before finishing his sentence. "That's stupid. I don't sulk. I just enjoy bothering Joslyn. She's an easy target."

"Yeah, okay." I shrugged, then sighed. "Look, I get it. You don't want to see your friend hurt."

"No, I don't want to see my sister hurt. I also don't want my sister to walk away from a good man just because she has reservations. I just think you should hear him out. Talk to him."

"We'll see." I bit my lip. "Like you said, I have to see him tomorrow anyway."

Chapter Twenty-Nine

Pilar

Sunday dinner was awkward for me. When the trumpets sounded out, and Benjamin Drake was presented, I didn't even look in that direction. In fact, I looked in the complete opposite one. I was trying to do as my brother had said. I was attempting to remember that Ben was human like the rest of us, and he *had* been trying to get ahold of me. I was attempting to not be upset about the fact that he'd hidden a son from me and an entire past that I should have been privy to. Why, though? Why should I have been privy to it? Because I was in love with him? I gasped inwardly. Was I in love with him? Instead of joining the crowd the way I normally did, I walked outside. Today's Sunday dinner was being held at Versailles. Quite fitting for a gossip mill. As I walked the grand halls and took the stairs quickly, I couldn't help but think about how many of my ancestors had suffered the same fate of trying to escape being the talk of the party. How many of them had run outside for fresh air to escape a lover's presence in Court?

It didn't matter. Unlike them, I didn't have an obligation to be here. I was here because it was my brother's first Sunday dinner, and Adeline had asked me to come. I was here because without this, I'd probably be in bed moping. And honestly, I needed to face Benjamin sooner rather than later. I just really, really didn't want to face him at all. I knew the moment I stood in front of him, I'd crumble. My heart would give in to his charms and good looks, and I'd bend to his will. But I couldn't. It was more than just the omission. I honest to God didn't think I could be with a father. A single dad. My heart broke even thinking about it. Not that he *was* a single father. I respected that, but I wasn't ready for what that would entail for me.

I was lost in thought and had reached the entrance to the labyrinth when I heard movement from behind me.

"Hey."

"Hey." I braced myself to face him. When I did, I realized that I hadn't prepared myself enough. I swallowed as he looked at me with a wariness I'd never seen on his face.

"I've been calling."

"I know."

"I've texted."

"I know."

"I miss you."

That one broke me. I swallowed again. "I'm mad at you."

"I know, and I'm sorry. I'm so terribly sorry." He reached for me. I pulled away, taking a step back.

"I'm not... I don't think I'm ready for this." I closed my eyes briefly. When I opened them again, he was just staring at me, the timidity turning to sadness.

"Because I have a son." He swallowed. I nodded.

"I'm so sorry."

"You don't have to apologize to me." He let out a laugh, raking his fingers through his curls. I wished so much that things were different so I could touch him. "I should have told you."

"You didn't think we were serious."

"Not in the beginning, but then..." He turned his face and stared off into the distance, the trees and land he could get lost in so easily.

"Then what?" I stepped forward.

"Then something happened. Something clicked." He shook his head, smiling over at me.

"Maybe it was too late when it happened. Perhaps I should have seen it sooner." He blinked, looking away again. "I guess it doesn't matter under the circumstances."

"I guess not," I whispered. My chest hurt as if my heart were hanging on by a string.

"Would things be different if I had told you?"

I bit my lip, shaking my head. "I don't think so."

"You're just not ready," he said with a nod as if understanding. "I wasn't either. I still don't know that I am. Parenthood is a funny thing."

"But he's yours, so you handle it."

"Exactly."

"I wish I wasn't so immature," I said over the knot in my throat.

"You're not immature, Pilar." He reached for me again. This time, I let him hold my hand in his even though his touch made me feel like I might break. "Not everyone is ready for this kind of commitment."

"I wish I was though."

"So do I." He squeezed my hand. "We had a good run though, yeah?"

"A very good run." There was no use trying to stop the tears from flowing down my face now. "I guess it was always supposed to come to an end."

"Maybe." He was trying to be empathetic, but I could tell he was just agreeing with me for the sake of agreeing. I cried harder, hating that I knew that about him. Instead of letting go of my hand, he pulled me into his arms and held me, setting his chin on my head and exhaling.

"Maybe another time will be the right time."

"Maybe." I sniffled against him, my heart breaking more as I spoke my next words. "Or maybe you'll find someone who's not scared of this kind of commitment and get married and forget about me."

His chuckle vibrated through me. "There's no chance I'll ever forget about you, Princess."

"I'll never forget you either." I pulled away, wiped my face, and took a deep breath as I looked into his deep hazel eyes, trying to memorize the moment.

Chapter Thirty

Ben had sent me flowers along with an apology letter when he found out that Kayla was responsible for slashing my tires. I heard he sent Aramis a ridiculously expensive bottle of scotch. I could only imagine how horrified he felt about the entire thing, even though it was not his fault.

It had been one week since I'd seen or heard from Ben, and I didn't know what to do with myself. It wasn't just sadness, it was despondence. I'd had a boyfriend for years before Ben, and I didn't feel this way when we broke up. These days, I felt like my heart was being ripped out of my chest. It took me three days to continue business as usual. I went to London with my mother and was currently helping Adeline put together a dinner party for Parliament.

"You realize you can hire someone to do this, right?" I asked for the third time since making our way around the flower shop.

"Obviously, Pilar. My mother owns an event planning business. I just want to make sure my vision is executed correctly."

"And you don't trust your mother to do that?"

She shot me a look. "I didn't say that."

"You sort of did."

"Just...look for bronze containers, for the love of God. And stop snapping at me."

"I'm not snapping at you." I frowned.

"You've been snappy all week. I understand you're going through a breakup, but it's a lot for all of us to handle."

"It's not...it's not technically a breakup."

"It's a breakup." She eyed me up and down. I looked down at myself. "What?"

"You're basically wearing pajamas out in the streets. I'm embarrassed."

"Embarrassed?" I gasped. "These are designer."

"Designer or not, they're still pajamas."

"You act like I'm wearing Crocs."

"God, please save us." She covered her face with her hand.

"I was barely with him, you know," I said finally. "I was with my ex much longer."

"I know."

"This feels like a slow death."

"Because you're in love with him."

I bit my lip. I'd come to that conclusion myself recently, but hearing it from someone else's lips made it real. I focused on finding the bronze vases and thought about that the rest of the time. Was love enough? Would love help me overcome the fear I had of not being enough for his son? I shook my head. I couldn't.

"Hey, P. I know this is bad timing and all, but there really isn't good timing for this," Adeline said as she crouched down to get a vase. She glanced up at me. "I'm pregnant."

"What?" The vases in my hand shook. "What?" I repeated.

"I'm pregnant." She stood up, smiling.

"Does my brother know?"

"He was there when I peed on the stick. Of course, he knows." She laughed. "But I figured you should get over your thing with kids soon. Say within the next seven months. Because, well, you're going to be an aunt."

I could only stare at her with my mouth ajar. Adeline pinched my cheek and kept shopping, leaving me standing there frozen. When my thoughts were no longer jumbled, I walked after her.

"Does Aramis know?"

"Not yet. I think Eli's telling him today."

"Do you know what you're having?" Suddenly I was smiling and excited. "Is it a girl?"

"We don't know yet." Adeline smiled wide. "Whatever it is, it'll be loved."

"Yes." I blinked. "It'll definitely be loved."

* * * *

I was just leaving the primary school I'd done today's rounds in when I spotted him—head full of curls, bright green eyes, and a smile that promised trouble. A pint-sized version of his daddy, but definitely his father's son. Amir and I shared a look, and I didn't have to tell him where my feet would lead me next. It wasn't like I'd planned this. I hadn't even known this was his school.

"Hey," I said to the boy.

"Hey." His eyes narrowed slightly. "You're my daddy's princess."

I let out what sounded like a strangled laugh. "I'm a princess, yes."

"Hmm." His lips moved when he made that sound, and a small dimple appeared. "Are you the reason he's sad?"

"What do you mean?"

"My dad. He's sad. I tried to give him ice cream but even that didn't cheer him up. I asked him if he still liked the princess and he looked even sadder." The boy pouted.

"I'm sorry he's sad," I whispered, kneeling down to eye level with him. "I bet he'll be happy soon."

"Not even my hugs are working." He shook his head. "And he says my hugs heal everything."

"I'm sorry."

"What's a princess doing in our school anyway?"

"Spending time with kids."

"Princesses like kids?" His brows rose.

"I guess they do."

"Kids like princesses." He smiled, the one that looked identical to his father's and made my heart melt.

"Do they?"

"I do."

"You do?" I felt myself smile wider. "Because they wait for their prince to rescue them?"

"Nah." He shook his head. "Daddy says princesses don't need saving."

"He said that?"

"He says they're the ones who do the saving."

"Really?"

"Yup." He frowned. "Do you think he's right?"

"I'm not sure." I sighed, repositioning myself so I was more comfortable. "What's your name?"

"Asher. Asher Drake," he announced proudly.

"I'm Pilar." I extended my hand to him. He took it in his small grip and bowed before kissing the backs of my fingers. I laughed.

"That was very official."

"I know. I saw it in a movie."

"You may just be my new favorite kid, Asher Drake."

"Does that mean I can be a knight?"

"Definitely."

"Will you knight me?" His eyes widened.

"Only the king can knight you." I winked. "It's a good thing I know him."

"Ash." The voice came from a woman, and we both turned in that direction. His mother. I stood quickly and patted his curls.

"It was great to speak to you, Asher."

"You too, Princess."

I felt a tiny rip in my heart then swallowed back the emotion that threatened to overwhelm me.

"I'm sorry. I was in the school and—" I began to apologize to his mother for speaking to her son, but she put a hand up and dismissed the apology.

"I'm glad you're here."

"Oh."

"It's not like I could exactly get ahold of you." She smiled. "And normally I wouldn't want to, but I know Ben, and I've never seen him this distraught."

"I'm sorry to hear that." I bit my lip.

"He told me it was because of this." She turned her head slightly toward Asher.

"It's not just this. It's not this at all actually." I smiled sadly. "It's me. I'm the problem."

"Because you don't think you're ready for this."

"I'm not."

"No one is. I mean, I don't think *I* am most days."

"That's what Ben said."

"He's not wrong," she said. "And my boyfriend, Jack, it's all new to him too, but he's trying, and he's doing so great." She paused, exhaling. "Anyway, I'm speaking out of turn, and I don't know your full story or issue. But I just want you to know that we're here for you. If you love Ben half as much as he loves you, we're all here for you."

The tears came then, even though I batted them away quickly. "He loves me?"

"He does."

"He said that?"

"He didn't have to." She smiled. "When you know, you know."

I licked my lips, nodding. "Thank you for this..."

"Tamara." She laughed. "I should have started with that. My name's Tamara."

"Thank you, Tamara. Truly." I looked at Asher again, who was now talking to the little boy beside him. "You've done an exceptional job with him."

"Thank you." She smiled and reached for her son's hand. "I hope to see you around."

I smiled but didn't say anything. I wasn't sure what I could say. I'd dismissed Ben and his feelings for me because I wasn't sure I was ready to assume a role in his child's life. Because I *wasn't* sure that I was prepared for that. I didn't know how to even speak to a child most of the time. I hadn't thought about Ben's feelings toward me or mine toward him. I hadn't thought about all of the extra stuff I'd be throwing away when I said goodbye to him. I hadn't taken into account the hollow feeling in my chest or how every single day would be consumed by thoughts of him. And I sure didn't know how to fix it now. But maybe it was time for me to step out of my comfort zone and try.

Chapter Thirty-One

Ben

The last thing I wanted to do was go out there and play a match, but I knew I had to. Between the Kayla thing weighing heavily on me, because I felt responsible for her being anywhere near Pilar in the first place, and letting go of Pilar, things were just not looking great for me. Football was my job though, and the show had to go on after Pilar. I'd only missed one game my entire career, and that was after my brother died.

"You've got this." David handed me my water bottle.

"I know." I nodded.

Even if I didn't have this, I would fake it until I made it. Sometimes it took that to get going, to get in the zone.

"Drake!" The voice came from behind me.

I turned around to see Warren Silva walking up. Now I definitely had to do my best out there. Silva was my idol, my mentor when I came into the league, and one of the best footballers to grace the pitch. I said hello to him, gave him a quick hug and dap.

"I didn't know you'd be here today."

"Camila wanted to take a trip to Paris, so here we are." He grinned.

"How's the baby?"

"Ah, you know how it is. He's hanging in there. We brought Camila's mom along with us to watch him while we do adult things."

"It's nice that you have that."

"It is. How are your parents?"

"They're great."

"Still in Israel?"

"Yeah, I'm trying to get them out here, but they keep saying they can't live away from the water."

"Ah, I bet it would be nice for them to be near Asher though."

"Well, they'll be here in a few weeks. Maybe if you're still here you can come over and help me convince them."

"I'd like that. We can smoke a cigar like old times." Warren chuckled. "Are they going to meet the princess when they're here, or is that old news?"

"I'm glad you're still reading tabloids." I was half-amused by this.

"You know I don't, but the monarchy is inescapable, even in the US."

"Well, no, they won't be meeting her. That's done."

"Damn, I thought maybe she'd be the one. You looked happy in the photos. Actually smiling for a change."

"I was. Happy, I mean." I felt myself smile now. As heartbreaking as the whole situation was, I was still grateful I'd had it. I just wished it didn't hurt so much to think about her now.

"I'm sorry it's over then." Warren looked like he wanted to ask questions but looked up and noticed the team was getting ready to run into the field, everyone standing by the kid they'd been assigned. He patted my back. "Good luck out there today, bro. Let's catch up after the game."

I ran over to the kid waiting for me and noticed I'd gotten a female this time. An adorable little girl who must have been around five years old, with big, brown eyes and long, brown hair. She almost looked like Pilar. This was definitely the universe's way of kicking my ass. She had a piece of paper in her free hand. A lot of the kids had brought things for us to sign. They were supposed to leave them behind, but we had no time for that, so I pretended I didn't see the paper. We walked onto the field, and the crowd roared. It was our first home game, and everyone was excited about it. Adrenaline soared through me, and I found myself vibrating along with their cheers. The little girl tugged my hand. I looked down and smiled at her, but she was handing me the paper.

"I can't sign it right now, sweetheart."

"It's not for you to sign. It's from the princess."

My heart stopped beating. I plucked the paper from her hand, let go of the other hand, and opened it up to see Pilar's handwriting staring back at me.

I can't say everything I want to say here, but I can say I'm sorry. I'll see you after the game. Love, Your Number 1 Fan, Pilar.

Could it be? She'd changed her mind? I read it again surrounded by the roaring crowd and felt myself nearly smile, but not quite. I knew Pilar wouldn't give this to me right before a big game if she didn't mean it, but her apology didn't mean she was taking me back. I looked out into the stands and suites where she'd most likely be, the smile intact on my face. Finally, I looked back at the little girl.

"She was at my school the other day. She's nice." She smiled too. "But I'm sorry to tell you, you're not a prince."

"I'm not." I chuckled.

"She says she doesn't need a prince."

"I bet she did."

"She said she needs a cute footballer." The little girl brought a hand up to cover her giggle right before she ran after the rest of the kids.

I couldn't help but laugh. I took the note in my hand and placed it in the tiny pocket inside the elastic of my shorts. I hoped the writing would still be legible after the game because I wanted to keep this forever.

Chapter Thirty-Two

Pilar

I waited outside. I didn't even know what to expect. I'd seen him smiling before the game as he read the note. I'd seen his gaze scanning the crowd as if he might find me in the sea of blue fans. I thought maybe if I tried hard enough, I could tell him where I was sitting, maybe connect our minds for the moment. Obviously, that didn't happen. This wasn't a romance movie. It was real life. And often, real love stories didn't play out the way we wanted them to. Sometimes there was no forgiveness or redemption. Sometimes there were only words of goodbye and other times, no closure at all.

I wasn't deluding myself into thinking he'd take me back just like that. It had only been a week and a half since we'd last seen each other. And sure, that time had been brutal, but maybe he'd realized that this wasn't worth it while we were apart. With me, he'd be in the public eye. Asher would be in the public eye now and would no longer have the anonymity he obviously craved, so I fully understood if he walked out here and told me to leave.

When he finally walked through the gates, I braced myself, swallowing hard and glancing at Amir as if this was one of the scenarios where he'd have to take a bullet for me. When he merely got into the driver's seat of the car and shut the door, that told me he wouldn't. This was a solitary fight, as wars of the heart often were. Ben had changed into his warm-up clothes, his hair still wet from a shower, and his swagger on one thousand as he walked over to me.

"I got your message." His expression was shuttered now, not euphoric like it had been before the game.

"And?"

"And." He set the designer duffel bag resting on his shoulder down on the ground. "I think it deserves a discussion."

"A heart-to-heart." I licked my lips, my hands shaky, suddenly nervous.

"If that's what you want to call it."

Oh God. I'd completely blown this. My chest hurt. I didn't know why I thought it would be easy. This was anything but. I felt like I was cutting myself open for him and he was just...neutral. Guarded. I didn't want him that way. I wanted him to feel as vulnerable as I did.

"So?" He raised an eyebrow.

"I..." I closed my eyes briefly. When I opened them again, he was still staring at me, and I thought...*to hell with it, what's the worst that can happen?* I took a deep breath. "I love you. I'm in love with you, and I have been for the longest time and—"

"How long?"

"What?"

"How long have you been in love with me?"

"I don't know. Does it matter?"

"It matters to me." He tilted his head slightly. "Were you in love with me the first night we hooked up?"

"Probably."

"Probably." He tore his gaze from mine and waved at someone behind me, probably one of his teammates since they all kept walking by, making this ordeal that much more mortifying for me.

"It doesn't matter. The point is that I am in love with you. I thought I wasn't ready for Asher, but...well, I'm ready for you, and you're a package deal, and I...I want to try. I understand if you're reluctant and don't want to bring other women around your son without having the certainty that they'll stick around, but I promise you that I will." I paused momentarily, taking in another gulp of breath. "I mean unless you don't want me to stick around. In which case, I won't. But that's all I had to say." I looked away because I could no longer bear to look at him.

He stepped closer and closer until he'd closed the distance between us, and he couldn't move another inch without slamming me against the car behind me.

"Look at me, Pilar."

I did, slowly bringing my gaze back to his, my heart slamming against my chest.

"I've been in love with you for so long, I couldn't even tell you when it happened. All I know is that I kept telling myself I wasn't, because I thought you'd never see me in that way. I'm just…I'm just a footballer. A nobody. I'm a poor boy from the wrong side of the tracks. I'm not an aristocrat. I thought I could have a normal, quiet life and not have my son involved in any of this, and I know that being with you means the opposite of that. Being with you will flip my world upside down. It will bring chaos and cameras and stories."

I bit my lip, looking down at my feet. This was exactly what I was afraid he'd say to me. He cupped my chin and tilted my face up so I had to look at him again.

"But if that's what being with you takes, I'll choose it every time. Because I love you. I love you, Princess. There's no one else I'd rather be with. There's no one I'd rather have my son around. There's nothing without you."

"Really?" I laughed, unable to help myself.

"Really."

"You love me?"

"So much, Princess." He pressed his lips against mine. "So much."

We kissed, standing in a deserted parking lot with only Amir and the other guards who were around watching. We stayed until the sun set with the promise that we'd take it one day at a time.

Together.

Chapter Thirty-Three

Ben

Pilar and I had been happily together for a couple of months now and everything had been blissful. It was one of the reasons my parents decided to fly into town and meet her. They claimed they were here to spend time with Asher, but I knew better, and I was grateful for it. I couldn't wait to introduce them to the woman in my life.

"Are you sure she likes Falafels?"

"I'm sure she'll like whatever you make, Mom."

"She's a princess, Benjamin. I don't know how to cook for a princess."

"Stop being dramatic." I threw my arms around my mother and squeezed her tight.

She'd been in the kitchen all day cooking for Pilar, who was set to come over for dinner to meet my parents and have a proper meal with Asher, Tamara, and Jack.

"Are you nervous?" My mother swatted me away with a wooden spoon.

"A little."

"Because of us?" Dad asked over the newspaper in his hands.

"Because of everything. I just want everyone to get along."

"Are you going to propose?" Dad raised an eyebrow.

Mom gasped, turning around. "You're going to propose?"

"Not tonight." I looked at both of them. "No talking about proposals."

"We can't talk about proposals, we can't talk about weddings, we can't ask if she wants children," Mom checked off. "What *can* we talk about, Benjamin?"

"Just normal stuff."

"She's a princess. I doubt she ever talks about normal stuff," Dad said. "What is normal stuff anyway?" He looked at the paper again. "Should I ask her why her brother is raising taxes?"

"God, no. Please no politics."

"We'll be mutes, Uri." Mom looked at Dad. "We'll be mutes."

"Better mutes now than mutes because our tongues got cut off by the king, Esther."

"He's not going to cut off your tongues." I closed my eyes briefly.

As much as I absolutely loved my parents, having them here every minute of the day was definitely testing my patience. It was the main reason I hadn't asked them to stay for once. I was grateful when the front door opened, and David walked in with a bottle of wine. He lifted it up.

"Brought wine instead of champagne. I wasn't sure if you were going to propose, but this was on sale, so I went with this."

"Jesus." I shook my head and turned around.

"See? Even David thinks you might propose," Mom said.

"I'm hoping you don't scare her off." I looked at the three of them, and back at the front door when it opened again and Tamara, Jack, and Asher walked in.

"Are we early?" Tam asked.

"You're fine." I waved a hand.

"We were just discussing Benjamin proposing to the princess," Mom said.

"You've got to be kidding me," I muttered.

"Is the princess going to be my stepmommy?" Asher asked excitedly, then looked back at his mother. "It's okay, Mommy, you'll always be my real mommy."

"I'm fully aware of that, Ash." Tamara laughed. "And quite frankly, I'm a bit excited about the princess joining our family." She winked at him and looked at me. "Are you proposing today?"

"No. No. No." I brought both hands up and looked at the ceiling. "Why is this happening?"

"I'll tell you what, if she sticks around after today's lunch, you should probably propose," Jack said, laughing.

"Brother, you read my mind." I looked at him and shook my head.

The doorbell rang, and that was when I froze. It was her. She'd been here a million times now. I'd given her a key to my place, and she'd given me one to hers. We'd been together officially for months, but she'd never been here when all of the most important people in my life were here. Suddenly I felt extremely nervous.

"Can I open it?" Ash asked, jumping up and down.

"Yes."

He ran over and opened the door, bowing. "Welcome, Princess."

She laughed. "Ash, you don't have to do that every time you see me."

I smiled wide at the sound of her voice. I hadn't even seen her yet, and my heart was already beating a mile a minute. When she did step inside with Amir in tow, she smiled at everyone. She crouched and hugged Asher first, giving him a kiss on the head. It'd been so beautiful to watch them together. For all of her reservations about children, Pilar treated Ash as if he were her own, and kept in touch with Tamara about everything. I'd always thought people with blended families were a little crazy. How could that ever work? But for us, it did. We all tried very hard to make it that way. Jack and I texted back and forth and watched some matches together. Tamara and Pilar had become friends because of Asher, but now spoke even when Asher wasn't involved. My mother and father shared a look that said they were weirded out by all of it but smiled, and I knew as strange as this was, they were proud. After Pilar said hello to Tam and Jack, she greeted David, and finally, walked over to me. It was obvious that she was nervous to say hi to my parents. I kissed her hard and grabbed her hand.

"Mom, this is Pilar. Pilar, this is my mother, Esther."

"So pleased to meet you, Esther." Pilar smiled and laughed when my mother pulled her into a hug.

"You're lovely. Thank you for coming over. I wanted to personally thank you for putting this goofy smile on my son's face," my mother said.

"Mom," I warned.

"You're blushing," Pilar said, laughing as she looked at me. "I didn't think that was possible."

"Stop." I looked away, knowing I was fully blushing, then looked back to introduce her to my father. "This is my father, Uri."

"So nice to meet you, Uri." Pilar smiled and hugged him as well.

Dad chuckled. "A hug from the princess!"

"Normally, I charge for those." Pilar winked.

"Oh? How much?" Dad cocked his head.

"I'm just kidding." Pilar laughed.

"Well, you should consider charging," Dad started.

"Next thing you know, he'll want to start taking care of your finances," David said, pointing at Dad. "Careful with that one."

"Nonsense." Dad waved him off. "I'm not a financial advisor, I'm a math professor who happens to know a lot about financial stability."

"I'll keep that in mind," Pilar said.

"Pilar, I have a new car." Asher ran up to her with the remote-control car my parents had given him. "Do you want to play?"

"Sure." She smiled. "After you eat your meal."

"Aw, man." He pouted, then smiled. "Okay, fine. I'm sitting next to you though."

"As long as your mom is okay with that," she said, running a hand through his hair.

I couldn't stop watching her. She was so good with everyone, and I knew without a doubt my parents loved her already. We spent the rest of the day eating and talking and playing with Asher. The only thing missing was my brother, but I knew deep down, he'd be happy for me as well.

Chapter Thirty-Four

Pilar

Much to our disbelief, Kayla had managed to get herself out of jail. Apparently, she had a rich boyfriend now, who paid for a great lawyer. The story was that there was no proof that she'd done what she had. There were no cameras in that area, and no witnesses. I had half a mind to pay a pretend witness, but I realized that was the kind of thing my father would have done, and the kind of thing we would spend the rest of our lives trying to clean up. Still, when I saw her walking toward me outside of the stadium, I let Amir take the lead.

"You need to stay twelve feet away from her," he said.

"Oh, I'm not here for her." Kayla frowned. "I'm over that. I've moved on."

"Yet, here you are." I waved in the direction of the stadium behind us.

"Only because my boyfriend owns the opposing team."

"Chelsea?" My eyes widened. "How you manage to land these men is an absolute mystery to me."

"I have what some call a golden vagina."

"Well, you should probably get that checked. It sounds like a medical condition."

"You had your moment, now you can leave," Amir said.

"It's fine." I waved a hand. "Hopefully we won't be seeing each other again anytime soon."

"Well, you're right about that. This is my last outing in Paris before I have to leave town for good, thanks to your brother." She shot me a look.

"I would apologize, but I'm not sorry for it. We don't like trash hanging around here." As I turned around with Amir in tow, I spotted two of our security walking up to her.

"She really isn't allowed anywhere near you," Amir said. "I guess she'll have to watch the game from the hotel or wait for her new boyfriend in London."

I laughed as we walked inside.

We watched the match, and thankfully Le Bleu beat Chelsea by two points—both scored by my boyfriend. He had me sitting on the field today in the owner's box. Generally I said no to that since I knew he hated the extra media attention, and this would definitely bring some on. Still, he'd asked, and I'd relented after telling him as much. He smiled and said that he was fine with the attention as long as I was there. At the end of the game, they had a ceremony to give out a plaque to a retired player, and Ben was front and center. I stood up and clapped and then Ben picked up the microphone and addressed the stadium, which was still a full house.

"I don't share much about my personal life with you, not because I don't love you, but because I didn't want it to overshadow my skills on the field," he said, "But today, I want to introduce my son, Asher." The crowd clapped and roared as Asher ran onto the field wearing his father's jersey—number four. "And as you all know, Asher and I have a very important person in our life, Princess Pilar." The crowd roared again. My heart pounded. What was he doing? "Asher and I were wondering if she'd join us out here."

"*What?*" I mouthed. I looked around everywhere, and my eyes landed on Amir, then on Elias beside him. And Aramis beside him with Adeline, Joss, Warren and Camila beside them. "What is going on?"

"Go!" they all signaled.

I saw Tamara and Jack and Ben's parents and my mother, and I couldn't wrap my head around it all, but my feet moved, and I walked out onto the field with the roar of the stadium driving me forward even faster. I couldn't imagine how it must feel to concentrate on playing out here. I covered my mouth as I reached Ben and Asher, who ran up to me to hug me.

"What are you doing, Benjamin?" I lowered my hand.

"Asher and I have a question that only you can answer," he said, still speaking into the microphone. I bit my lip as he leaned down to include his son in on the speech, and then Ben said, "Will you marry me?" as Asher asked, "Will you marry my dad?"

I laughed, covering my face with both hands as I started to cry and nod, and cry and nod some more, and laugh.

Ben took out a box and got on one knee in front of me, giving the microphone to Asher so this part wasn't publicized.

"I never thought I'd be the kind of man who would want to settle down with someone, and I know you had your reservations about me and the baggage I brought with me as well, but this last year with you has been the best of my entire life. I don't want it to ever end. I will never stop being in love with you, Princess. Marry me. Please." He smiled up at me. I nodded some more.

"Yes."

He slid the ring onto my finger, a beautiful oval, diamond-encrusted ring that, like Ben, was so much more than I'd ever imagined. He stood up and hugged me, lifting me off the ground as I kissed him. Asher jumped up and down, cheering along with the crowd in the stadium. It was, by far, the most perfect moment I'd ever experienced.

Sign up for the 1001 Dark Nights Newsletter
and be entered to win a Tiffany Key necklace.

There's a contest every month!

Go to www.1001DarkNights.com to subscribe.

**As a bonus, all subscribers can download
FIVE FREE exclusive books!**

Discover 1001 Dark Nights Collection Seven

For more information, go to www.1001DarkNights.com

THE BISHOP by Skye Warren
A Tanglewood Novella

TAKEN WITH YOU by Carrie Ann Ryan
A Fractured Connections Novella

DRAGON LOST by Donna Grant
A Dark Kings Novella

SEXY LOVE by Carly Phillips
A Sexy Series Novella

PROVOKE by Rachel Van Dyken
A Seaside Pictures Novella

RAFE by Sawyer Bennett
An Arizona Vengeance Novella

THE NAUGHTY PRINCESS by Claire Contreras
A Sexy Royals Novella

THE GRAVEYARD SHIFT by Darynda Jones
A Charley Davidson Novella

CHARMED by Lexi Blake
A Masters and Mercenaries Novella

SACRIFICE OF DARKNESS by Alexandra Ivy
A Guardians of Eternity Novella

THE QUEEN by Jen Armentrout
A Wicked Novella

BEGIN AGAIN by Jennifer Probst
A Stay Novella

VIXEN by Rebecca Zanetti
A Dark Protectors/Rebels Novella

SLASH by Laurelin Paige
A Slay Series Novella

THE DEAD HEAT OF SUMMER by Heather Graham
A Krewe of Hunters Novella

WILD FIRE by Kristen Ashley
A Chaos Novella

MORE THAN PROTECT YOU by Shayla Black
A More Than Words Novella

LOVE SONG by Kylie Scott
A Stage Dive Novella

CHERISH ME by J. Kenner
A Stark Ever After Novella

SHINE WITH ME by Kristen Proby
A With Me in Seattle Novella

And new from Blue Box Press:

TEASE ME by J. Kenner
A Stark International Novel

FROM BLOOD AND ASH by Jennifer L. Armentrout
A Blood and Ash Novel

QUEEN MOVE by Kennedy Ryan

The Sinful King
An Enemies to Lovers Standalone Romance
By Claire Contreras
Now Available

From *New York Times Bestselling* Author, Claire Contreras, comes a new, sexy, 100% stand-alone novel...

If you had any ties to Marbella, it was impossible for you not to have heard the stories about Prince Elias and his debauchery.

Every summer he arrived with his security detail and friends in tow and rented out a row of cottages near the water.

Cottages that belonged to my family.

Each of those summers, my parents sent me away – summer camp and later, boarding school. Anything to keep me away from the royals and their partying.

I hadn't been home in years, but when I finally come back for the summer, I see that not much has changed. Like all the summers I'd been gone, Prince Elias is back, but this time with an incognito security detail and no friends. This time, there is no partying, no noise, no crowds. No reason at all to even think he was there.

I'm given strict orders not to talk to him, not to even look in his direction, but he makes this an impossible task. I may be doing everything in my power to stay away from him, but there is no one in the world who can say no to the future King of France.

* * * *

"Did my party bore you?"

My heart stopped beating as my eyes popped open. I turned my face and looked up. Prince Elias seemed impossibly tall from this angle, like a giant who could touch the sky. Maybe he could. He sat down beside me, slipping the mask from his face and tossing it on the sand. Glancing over my shoulder, I could see his security detail standing by the steps. Near, yet far enough to give him privacy. I wondered if he'd bring up what just happened inside. I wondered if I would. No. Forget about it. It was a mistake. A one-time thing that happened at a sexy party. Nothing else.

"Did it bore you?" I asked after a beat.

"I'm here, aren't I?"

"You make it sound like this may not be that much better." My lip tilted at that. "You really are an asshole, you know that?"

"So you've said."

"I'm sure I'm not the only one who's brought that to your attention." I glanced at him. He had his long arms set on his knees, his hands dangling as he looked out into the ocean.

"Outside of my siblings and maybe a few cousins, you are the only one who's said it to me." He met my gaze after a moment. "To my face, anyway."

"Interesting."

"It is interesting." He inched closer. "Do you know why they won't say it to my face?"

"They're afraid of the consequences?"

"I guess so. I could end them. Easily."

"Perks of being the future king."

"There aren't many perks to that job." He made a sound that sounded between a snort and a scoff as he looked away from me. I stared at his profile. He had pretty features. Rugged yet pretty.

"There might be if your family wasn't dead set on keeping things so traditional."

"You think I haven't had this conversation countless times?" He looked at me again. "Do you think I haven't tried to figure out ways to keep the Crown happy and the people happy? It's not as simple as you may think it is."

"You're right. I don't imagine it is."

"It's a lot of pressure. The king dying."

"Your father, you mean."

"My father, the king." His eyes searched mine. "I don't expect you see him as a father or a husband. Just as a strict ruler who wants the last say in everything and the reason a lot of people are suffering."

This time, I glanced away and looked back at the ocean. The turmoil in it matched his eyes, and I couldn't seem to find solace in it. He wasn't wrong. A lot of people were waiting for his father's demise. There were hungry people in the street. People losing their houses, their jobs, their families. It wasn't something the king could possibly understand and up until tonight, something I didn't think Prince Elias could understand either. Maybe I'd been wrong in my judgment. He seemed like a man who carried loss well, but felt the burden of it nonetheless. The sound of sand swishing behind us made us turn our heads as one of his security detail approached.

"The Princess of Austria is looking for you," he said.

Prince Elias sighed heavily, throwing his head back as if to ask the universe for patience. It was yet another glimpse of the person he hid beneath his stoicism. He stood up slowly, the sand on his pants falling on the skirt of my dress with the movement. The security detail walked away and Prince Elias stood there for a long moment in silence, watching the ocean, with only the sound of the waves to disturb his thoughts.

"I'll see you another time, Miss Adeline," he said. "Thank you for indulging me and attending the party, as short-lived as it was."

About Claire Contreras

Claire Contreras is a *New York Times* Best Selling Author. Her books range from romantic suspense to contemporary romance and are currently translated in over fifteen languages.

She's a breast cancer survivor, a mother, a wife, and a Florida girl that currently resides in Charlotte, NC. When she's not writing, she's usually lost in a book.

Sign up for RELEASE DAY ONLY text alerts by texting BOOK to 21000.

Sign up for her monthly newsletter (which doesn't really come every month): https://www.subscribepage.com/ClaireContrerasNewsletter

FB GROUP:

https://www.facebook.com/groups/ClaireContrerasBooks/

Website: http://www.clairecontrerasbooks.com/

Twitter: @ClariCon

Instagram: ClaireContreras

Discover 1001 Dark Nights

For more information, go to www.1001DarkNights.com

CIPHER by Larissa Ione
RESCUING MACIE by Susan Stoker
ENCHANTED by Lexi Blake
TAKE THE BRIDE by Carly Phillips
INDULGE ME by J. Kenner
THE KING by Jennifer L. Armentrout
QUIET MAN by Kristen Ashley
ABANDON by Rachel Van Dyken
THE OPEN DOOR by Laurelin Paige
CLOSER by Kylie Scott
SOMETHING JUST LIKE THIS by Jennifer Probst
BLOOD NIGHT by Heather Graham
TWIST OF FATE by Jill Shalvis
MORE THAN PLEASURE YOU by Shayla Black
WONDER WITH ME by Kristen Proby
THE DARKEST ASSASSIN by Gena Showalter

Discover Blue Box Press

TAME ME by J. Kenner
TEMPT ME by J. Kenner
DAMIEN by J. Kenner
TEASE ME by J. Kenner
REAPER by Larissa Ione
THE SURRENDER GATE by Christopher Rice
SERVICING THE TARGET by Cherise Sinclair

On Behalf of 1001 Dark Nights,

Liz Berry, M.J. Rose, and Jillian Stein would like to thank ~

Steve Berry
Doug Scofield
Benjamin Stein
Kim Guidroz
InkSlinger PR
Dan Slater
Asha Hossain
Chris Graham
Chelle Olson
Kasi Alexander
Jessica Johns
Dylan Stockton
Richard Blake
and Simon Lipskar

Made in the USA
Columbia, SC
08 May 2020